G000131323

Brian Barr's
The King in Yellow

Four King in Yellow Stories
Written by Brian Barr

Edited by Jeff O' Brien

Cover Art by Don Noble

Table of Contents

A Visage of Great Truths

"Oscar to Epic 7, come in. I repeat, come in. Have you found more wreckage?"

"Looks like an entire wreckage of various crafts, Oscar." Deborah moved calmly through the alien landscape with her colleague, suited up in their protective ivory suits. She was fascinated with the strange lavender hues on the towering rocks, waves of dried lake beds, and what looked to be devastated dome buildings and crashed extraterrestrial space ships. "Would take a lot of crews to come up here and bring them home for research."

"And do they bear that weird symbol?"

"The squiggly yellow thing? Yeah, it's all over the place. Not just on the interiors of broken shells like we found before. We see it on the outside of ships as well. What the hell does it mean?"

"Top secret. You just report what you see, and keep your cameras on."

"Yeah, yeah."

Everything was top secret. Ground control never shared anything with their subordinate astronauts, lackies they sent to and fro to investigate far off terrains. Finding these weird ships with that strange symbol on them seemed pretty important to the American Space Program. If the ships were really top secret, maybe they had made a mistake in letting the damned space vehicles get shown on the news.

Ever since that one broadcast, however, they had been careful not to let any other footage of the strange symbol get out in public. They just wanted Deborah, Will, and all their other astros to find, document, and gather whatever they could, then bring it back to base.

"We'll really need a big team to gather all of this, Oscar," Will reminded ground control as he picked up a lightweight metal, stained with yellow on its shell. "Unbelievable how much stuff is up here. Like some lost empire."

The first people to reach an exoplanet, and no one would hear about it. Deborah wouldn't be paraded on broadcasts, or honored as one of the first humans, or the first woman astronaut, who walked along the surface of a planet outside of the Solar System. No; Oscar wanted everything secret. Private. No one was to know of their feat, of how they came here, or why. Why this planet, exactly, of all the various exoplanets ASP had discovered through telescopic research? Why here?

Deborah glanced up from the wreckage, her mouth dropping inside of her bulky helmet. "Will, look up."

A light was shining, perhaps twelve feet overhead. A brilliant, yellow light, almost golden, yet so anemic and pallid. No feelings of warmth or happiness came from it. Instead, the light was accompanied with a strong wave of dread, an absolute tinge of chaos.

"My God," Will whispered into his helmet's microphone.

In a circle, eleven other pale yellow lights appeared at a circumference of eight to ten feet, each bringing an aroma and presence of doom and despair. They were a little taller than a natural human, perhaps twelve to thirteen feet tall, so intimidating. Powerful winds began to glow, dust rising from the planet's surface as Will and Deborah began to back up.

"What the hell is going on up there?" Oscar asked frantically. "Epic 7? Epic 7?"

On the shrapnel of fallen spacecraft, the yellow markings all began to glow. Whether they glowed on their own or by the brilliance of the overhead lights, neither Deborah nor Will knew for certain, or even thought to question. The lights were descending, and they were taking shapes, forming faces, gaining limbs, at times humanoid, at times not.

As if a fist had closed around it, Deborah and Will's own shuttle, parked a quarter of a mile away, was suddenly crushed. It shattered into pieces as stealth glass, wires, and metal broke, gas chambers exploding in wild blazes. Fire shot upwards as Will and Deborah looked behind them, eyes wide, mouths agape. Even the heat radiating from the destroyed vessels couldn't penetrate the eerie dread of the yellow lights, lacking any sense of temperature, warm or cold.

Deborah and Will screamed for ground control, their connection lost.

The lights stood at ground level now, their descent finished. Cold stares exuded from the morphing faces they wore.

The strangers advanced towards them. Both astronauts stopped screaming as their suits imploded against their helpless flesh, yellow enveloping them.

***

"Does he ever show his face?"

Maddie glanced up from the picture of The Yellow Sign sprawled upon the cold basement floor in chalk, five cadavers encircling the cryptic symbol with fresh gore and blood. Crimson sanguine fluid linked the corpses in their circle, pouring in long, interconnected lines.

How could Maddie answer Raymond's simple question? In ways, yes, The King in Yellow did show his grand, magnificent face, but not as obviously as new, ignorant initiates may have expected. There was the Pallid Mask, and there was the Golden Woman, the Worshipping Apparitions, many more representations of The King. They were all reflections or angels, ambassadors, possibly even avatars, of his most high brilliance.

But *the* face? Who was to say? The King was a mystery beyond mysteries. He was eternal decadence and destruction. Destruction was creation, and creation was destruction.

"He reveals himself in a variety of ways," Maddie finally answered to his apprentice, "but we are not to question, or even wonder, how He presents Himself. We must always remember He is beyond our comprehension or understanding, and always beyond our humanity, lest we end up as fools like Hildred and all the others. He is King and we are not. Do not forget our task, Raymond. Our task is to go wild, to obey the madness The King has bestowed upon us, and to work our art in His name."

Raymond, Maddie's apprentice, stared at his hands and the long dagger they held. The blood still stained them, and sullied his clothing as well. "Must we always do such dreadful things to gain his favor? Believe me, I meant it when I said I wished to worship him, to serve him, ever since I saw that sign, but-"

"Your faith can't be so weak. Not now."

Maddie tried to be forgiving to his younger apprentice. 2020 had been a cruel year for the both of them, though Maddie had known worse times, an entire decade Raymond couldn't have even imagined. Raymond was a young comedic actor who hadn't worked on a play in over a year, ever since he joined Maddie on his quest. The young man had confided in Maddie, telling him that he had seen The Yellow Sign *before* it had reappeared on that news broadcast, in a series of dreams before he discovered it on buried digital links.

The actors first physically met through a Shakespearean theatrical company in New York, eventually deciphering that they had encountered each other's handles on some underground DigiWeb forum related to The Yellow Sign. Raymond had told Maddie he found traces of news footage online, showing the same previously live event that uncovered the American Space Program's discovery of The Yellow Sign on mysterious spacecraft. When Raymond had seen that footage, he was shocked to see the very symbol that had plagued him in cryptic dreams was proven to be real. The actor was inspired to investigate the symbol further, understanding that this information was strangely suppressed by the very agencies that had released the information.

Once comfortable that Raymond was safe, Maddie told Raymond of his work, and sent him a document of *The King in Yellow* play via DigiMail. Thus began a long, wondrous relationship, collaborations mixed with murder, magic, and mayhem. How fortunate they were to work this long together, evading the watchful eye of the law. Maddie thanked The King, his great deity whose ambassadors assured that Raymond was to be trusted and used in his operations.

Sometimes Maddie felt bad for inviting Raymond on this path, for possibly not describing how much would need to be sacrificed or given in order to gain the great deity's favor. They shared death together, and blood stained both pairs of their hands. They had brought suffering to many people, but the hell they endured was only an extension of The King's power.

"Once you read the play," Maddie continued, cleansing the sabre in his hands as he walked away from the circle, "you opened the gateway. You cannot stop now, and to cease in the great work would be to incur the wrath of The King. As you know, the show must go on."

"I would never stop," Raymond reassured. He placed his dagger on a nearby table and picked up a thurible, burning the charcoal inside of it before placing lavender leaves and frankincense clusters upon it. "Believe me. I am loyal to The King in all of my endeavors, Maddie, and I'd hate to disappoint you."

"You have no need to worry about disappointing *me*. The King smiles upon artists and scholars. Remember that." Maddie sighed as he picked up his ceremonial sword. The fool had a lot to learn, and he was as dimwitted as the clowns he portrayed in those classic plays. "Now, you set everything up. I'll prepare myself. I'll also need to check everything upstairs, make sure the blinds are drawn, that the doors are properly locked and the mirrors are turned to face the walls, unless we want to be disturbed."

"Of course," Raymond answered, returning to his tools.

This ritual meant a great deal to the both of them. That glorious May, the sun was in Hyades, along with Saturn and Mars as well. Though it was black down in that basement, accompanied only by the glow of candles, the outside world was glorious, bathed in Spring light, a sylvan scene illuminated even in those dark times. There in the protection of a beautiful New England countryside, a skilled magi and his learning apprentice dedicated themselves to a mighty task. Other artists, inventors, and eccentrics had been chosen throughout the past century, and centuries before, to bring The King's Imperial Dynasty of America to fruition on Earth. In the end, human flaw brought the predecessors down, made them ruin their monarch's plans. Ego, vanity, laziness, greed, so many vices of unworthy acolytes had stalled the full beauty their great monarch could bring to their world.

Maddie was confident that where those past, ignorant artists had failed, he and Raymond would succeed.

***

Maddie met The King in Paris.

From the first moment he opened the pages of *The King in Yellow*, that accursed play, he was held, transfixed. All of his life, he had performed in what he thought were the greatest plays, all of them Shakespearean, from Macbeth to King Lear, yet that play was beyond even the world's most renowned playwright.

No wonder it was now illegal. The illegality of the text only encouraged Maddie to find it. Ever since the American Space Program brought back strange shrapnel from space with The Yellow Sign, broadcasting it globally nearly ten years ago, Maddie wanted to know exactly what that symbol meant. Where did it come from, who created it? Was it extraterrestrial beings that spray-painted the damned thing on their ships, or failed human astronauts going mad in the vacuums of space?

Maddie's search took him to the library, to the DigiWebs, searching for keywords like "Yellow Sign" and "Strange Marks". Links upon links came back, and after weeks of perusing, he fell upon a secret, forgotten history. Wars. Séances. The Yellow Sign. The Pallid Mask.

The King in Yellow.

Many had worshipped him. People fell under his sway, entering some sort of divine madness, and all thanks to a play that had been mass marketed, sold internationally. Asylums were filled, suicides rampant. Governments began to ban the work, starting with the United States. But he had to find it, through those tomes of books. That decadent splendor remained with him since he found and read the play, guiding him without fail.

A book that destroyed all deceptions, revealed all hidden realities, each one revolving around, extending from, and composed of His Grace, The King in Yellow. The world was not as Maddie once believed it to be, not limited by mud and water, as constructed as the brick and mortar made by man. Nature was a charade, a farce, clay in the hands of beings beyond his comprehension. Through veiled language, representational characters, and staged scenes, the play described every aspect of existence as created and ruled by The King in Yellow. Few surmised what Maddie did, that every aspect of that script shed light on The King, always going back to him, from his feminine aspects to his masculine, his lighter properties and attributes to his most darkest components. Maddie feared the play, and adored it. The holy text opened worlds for him, sent him places in his sleep and deep meditations, moving aboard strange vessels and chariots through the stars.

Maddie remembered the first time he entered those strange worlds, confirming what he knew since he found that text, that The King was *real*. As his body slept, Maddie's soul shot through the heavens at warped speed. Ushered to the constellation of Taurus, he met the mysterious ones, servants of His Majesty. Guided by those strangers hooded in yellow lights, he traveled on strange, enigmatic vessels that looked nothing like the naval ships and even the space ships found at home, far more advanced. He traveled along Lake Hali, seeing its strange, toxic purple waters under dark, foggy green skies. Cold, whipping winds stung his face as they rushed by like sprinting horses. Twin suns were anchoring themselves into the waters, far in the distance. Along those coasts, the animated skeletons of wolves ran alongside lynxes in wild packs, howling occasionally. Owls fluttered and hooted from rotting branches. Maddie saw wraiths of dead alien creatures wavering between the dead trees and colorful rocks, walking through gray grass as they worshipped the black stars overhead. Aldebaran and the Hyades embodied hell above them, penetrating the thickness of those lead clouds, and Maddie swore he could hear each shimmering star sing. All apparitions exalted the astral guardians with barbarous chants. For all time, they had and would worship those stars. They knew the dread, feared it, and respected it.

"Fear is respect," one of the yellow hooded ambassadors had said, "and respect is fear. Fear is the threshold of destruction. Destruction is creation, and creation is destruction."

Maddie remembered the fright penetrating him, hearing that ancient one speak in his bastard English language. He knew, then and there, that they could hear his every thought, feel his every emotion, and he was at their mercy.

Further up the lake they went, until they reached the horrid necropolis of Carcosa. What a strange and melancholic city, with towering buildings made of material Maddie didn't even recognize, reeking of carrion.

"Will I see The King here?" Maddie asked.

"No one sees The King. Not directly. You must be content in the ways you see him now. In everything you see."

"And what about you? Can I see your faces, who you really are? Haven't I worked hard enough for that pleasure?"

"You will not see us in our truest form."

"Why not?"

"Because to see us would mean your ultimate destruction. You have work to do before you are granted that honor."

Maddie hushed from that moment, realizing that he was too close to overstepping his boundaries. That was how many previously chosen servants had failed, allowing their egos to overstep the edicts of

The King, feeling entitled to mysteries beyond their comprehension. No, he would not pry; he would follow and listen.

Docking their ship, the yellow ones took him through the city. They showed him the great monoliths, the mighty architecture, and horrendous roads. Black skyscrapers, with sharp peaks, served vigil over the cracked streets. A macabre populace of ghosts and other dead creatures slithered through the alleyways like serpents, heads low and ashamed. They were antisocial to each other, far removed even in their gatherings, lost in the demanding worship of death and chaos. No one's presence in Carcosa could override the desolated, isolated feel of the dark metropolis. This was truly a ghost city, ruins that stood tall as an arena of devastation, and Maddie realized with dread that he was the only living thing there.

Everywhere, The Yellow Sign stood proudly, shining, forever reminding the denizens of who owned them. The King's castle was most frightening, its turrets corroded in mismatched black and yellow, The Yellow Sign flying proudly from black flags atop sharp coned towers stretching to the sky. Within that dark building, the ambassadors took him to the grand palace, and Maddie even saw the doors of the throne room. He didn't have to ask if they could be opened.

From outside the throne room Maddie was led down a long hall, taken into a meeting room. The yellow hooded beings took him to a long table with The Yellow Sign sprawled upon its top.

They all sat. Maddie waited patiently as the beings looked back and forth to each other, speaking in their ancient language. Who knew what they were discussing, secrets they didn't even share with this selected acolyte from Earth.

Finally, one of them spoke. "You have been granted the privilege to see our world. To enter the city of Carcosa, to enter the royal palace. With your loyalty and humility, The Imperial Dynasty of America will be realized. Your world can know grace, under a united world, ruled by The King in Yellow."

"Your world has been ruled by your inadequate race for too long," interjected another. "Fragile minds, infantile egos, men bent on greed, prejudice, and power. They don't understand fear, or respect truth, feigning religious values that they use to control and subjugate people they see as being beneath them. Very few people on your planet understand their self worth."

"The fear of The King in Yellow shall be placed upon them. All of them. As we have done in many worlds past, in many ways, for endless decades."

"But why can't The King in Yellow come on his own merit?" Maddie asked curiously. "Why does he need someone as low as me to help him realize his kingdom on Earth?"

"The veils of illusion are thick in your world," one answered. "Your planet, like many, is light years away, lost in the darkness of mundane ignorance. Through the ancient arts, you can uplift the veils that keep us separated. You can part light years of distances by milliseconds, as easily as you can travel in your dreaming. You can bring the reality of our King and His Kingdom to the people of your planet."

He had won The King's favor. Maddie would come back to Carcosa many times after that, his sleep relieving his soul of his body, allowing him to travel with the aid of the yellow servants. He followed them, and listened, agreeing to the tasks they set aside for him to do.

After seven macabre, demented years in Europe, bonding with The King and doing his bidding through many a blood sacrifice in France, Italy, and Spain, Maddie came back to the States. Never did a fear of getting caught enter his mind - The King was beyond forensic science, detectives, and the law in general. Maddie conducted his great work without interruption. He would do anything to make his monarch physically manifest in that world, to destroy the illusion of the false reality most humans consumed themselves with ignorantly. Soon, they would all cower, all tremble in fear at the decadent splendor of the Pallid Mask. They would shake, scream, and remember, united in unison by the divinity of pain.

***

Maddie placed the weighted diadem upon his head, golden and shimmering with diamonds. A powerful accessory, that crown, one that few were humble enough to wear. Maddie had to remember, even as a chosen servant of The King, he could never *be* The King. Wearing this physical accessory was a privilege, not a right, and he wore it for his God.

The fine silk white robe bearing The Yellow Sign came next. On Maddie's frail, saturnine figure, the opulent robe looked quite bulky on him, but it didn't matter. He wasn't wearing the grand clothing for himself, and he would remain humble.

He also had to stay humble in working with the apprentice The King had picked out for him. How hard he had to suppress that judgmental side that wanted to scream against having a partner, let alone Raymond. Maddie found Raymond dull, ignorant, and slightly depressing to deal with. He was often having to remind Raymond to set up the proper tools, how to abduct their victims, how to murder them, etc.

In training Raymond, Maddie's own practice and training was brought into question. For the near decade he had scoured through Europe, learning of occult practices and operations from books and other skilled experts, he had secretly devoted himself to The King in Yellow. If the esoteric organizations he had joined knew how he had used his very training for blood rituals and deadly sacrifices, he doubted any of them would have been pleased with how he used his occult education. Their opinions didn't matter to him. Only The King in Yellow's divine favor mattered.

The time was right for the ultimate ritual, where Raymond and Maddie's skills would truly be put to the test. Cruel Taurus spread its deviance overhead, the sun highlighting the constellation with exuberance. That stubborn bull, its hidden darkness flowing through those stars of the Hyades and the Pleiades, ruler of spring, lazy in appearance yet boiling to the brim with madness and demonic principles. The constellation was home to The King, his gaze silently ruling at its heights from the ends of April to the beginnings of May, The Yellow Sign strongest in this time period.

Fully clothed and prepared, Maddie walked out of his dressing room. His robe dragged as he moved towards the basement, the diadem surprisingly heavy on his head. The crown had been forged ages ago by worshippers of the yellow, the robe only a few centuries old and surprisingly preserved.

Maddie's hand opened the basement door. He could smell the incense so strong in clouds of reverence, the darkness pervading. Down the stairs he descended, his mind focused, passions cast aside. Only The King consumed his thoughts, the strong smells of rotting flesh and slaughtered human meat ignored.

Finally, Maddie reached the basement floor. The candles burned bright as Raymond sat atop the corpse in the circle of other cadavers, his head swooning back and forth, The Yellow Sign drawn beneath him. The bloody circle stained around the corpses was creating a variety of symbols that came and went like the ebb and flow of the moon, inscriptions that disappeared as soon as they were formed.

Maddie cringed as the blood turned yellow, resembling rich piss. The smell of gore intensified, vibrations of dread awakened throughout the room.

"Come forward," Raymond said in a voice that wasn't his own.

Maddie recognized one of the voices of the Carcosan ambassadors, one of the yellow beings from his soul travels. He stepped forward, opening, his head lowered as the crown shined upon his head.

"Kneel," said the voice as Maddie just reached the outside of the yellowed circle.

Falling upon one knee, Maddie continued to look at the floor. He shook in the wave of desolation rushing at him like freight trains, the entire room possessing a flaxen glow.

Foreign chants started to spew from Raymond, whom Maddie now realized was as dead as the corpse under him and the bodies surrounding him. Light enveloped Raymond's body as he spewed those alien mantras. More chants joined in unison throughout the room, and soon, eleven more lights appeared, surrounding Maddie, standing taller than human heights were fathomable.

After a lost track of time, kneeling there and hearing those gothic voices, the chanting stopped. Silence followed for only a moment, before the yellow being possessing Raymond announced, "a new age has dawned upon your planet. For centuries, The King has devised to expand his dynasty here, a world that has always been secretly under his control. Now, the veils are removed, and his might can be established beyond the physical illusions that have blocked his full potential."

Underneath that horrid dread Maddie felt, an even greater feeling of accomplishment and pride couldn't help but to burst forth from his heart. He had done it. Succeeding where others had failed, he had ushered in a new era. The King's might, his grand reign, would be felt throughout the corners of the Earth. Mankind would bow and know the significance of The Yellow Sign. Their eyes would turn to the stars of Taurus and know the true ruler of that infinite expanse called space, the planets and inferior stars held within it. Heads would fall, downcast in humility and shame, hands extended in praising prayers, hearts pulsing in constant, unending trepidation.

"Show him," one of the yellow said to its brethren. "He deserves that much."

Deserves what? Maddie wondered in excitement. *Have they chosen me worthy to see that face, the grand face that has eluded many others for centuries, millenniums-*

Maddie's thoughts froze as the room dissipated around him. Yellow was everywhere, and the basement, even Maddie's mansion, seemed nonexistent around him. No signs of those New England woods surrounded him, no leaf of grass, no blue skies overhead. He seemed to not recognize his Earth, nor was he in Carcosa, where even the realities of death were apparent. Here, no reality but The King was apparent, and various shapes, forms and faces morphed in and out around him, teasing him, drawing his attention closer. All illusions, however, were as ephemeral as the world Maddie had once known.

Destruction was kind after Maddie gazed upon the truth. With that great truth revealed, he saw, feared, and respected the eternity of The King in Yellow.

The Sacred House

Marty and his friends finally got the house's residents squared away.

The task took long enough. Smashing into the house was easy, breaking through the windows and scaring the living daylights out of the family living there. Wearing all black, they were six in all, big men in ski masks who found it easy to intimidate and overpower the four-member family. From the father and mother to the daughter and son, everyone was subdued, screaming and kicking in their ropes with great terror as Samson and Raymond aimed guns at their heads.

"Tell them to shut the fuck up down there!" Marty shouted as he, Marshall, Lou, and Ben continued to rummage through the house, grabbing anything of value. From gold necklaces to watches and electronics, the home invaders were taking anything they could find. They had a big truck to haul as much as they wanted out of that big, fancy looking house in the middle of the country, and it wouldn't take long to get out of there.

Marty and Marshall found a safe in the dad's study. What an interesting room, the walls hidden by bookshelves, filled with classic collections of Shakespeare, Poe, Lovecraft. The man obviously had an interest in literature, and by the looks of some other books, a great love for theatre as well. There were books on acting, pantomiming, stage presence and famous movies.

There was a time when Marty wanted to be an actor; a long time ago, when he first moved to California. He didn't live in the north of the state at that time, swallowed by that great eye magnet, Los Angeles. Though he tried to make it, tried to stand out as a phenomenal force of theatre, something about him prevented Marty from reaching his star. He wasn't handsome enough, wasn't talented enough, wasn't enchanting enough...

Then came the ice addiction. Meth was his friend. From meth and a heavy need of drugs came connections to biker gangs, to the wrong side of the law. It wasn't long before Marty was breaking the law himself, was driving up and down California with the wrong crowds looking for get rich quick schemes to blow the earnings on ice. Before he knew it, Marty was an all-out criminal.

His addiction would take him down. He knew it. With each stolen device, each cracking safe...

And what a safe they found in this man's study, this place out in the country. It would take a while to break in, but with a crowbar, some force, and diligence, Marty and Marshall soon found the safe door opening...

To their surprise there was a great deal of money in there. This country bastard and his family were rich! Stacks upon stacks of hundreds. There were also jewels, more necklaces, more watches, diamonds and gold...

And a book. A strange book resting on top of all that money.

Marty picked up the book and looked at it. On top of that cover was a weird, squiggly sign.

A yellow sign.

"Holy fuck," Marshall said with a grin as he picked up one stack of notes, then another, slinging it into his already stuffed back. "How much money do you think is in here, Marty? This is crazy!"

Marty was too interested in that book, his mind moving away from the money, just for a moment. Why would such a book be thrown into this safe, away from the other books on the shelves? With interest, Mary cracked open the strange text.

Some play. Acts, characters, prop listings, masks descriptions. What a strange play, with such strange words. Carcosa, Lake Hali, Aldebaran, the Bull of Heaven...

"Dude, what the fuck are you looking at?" Marshall asked, his voice pulling Marty from his trance. "Grab the loot, let's get the fuck out of here!"

A shot rang out from the basement.

Marty and Marshall turned their heads.

"Fuck," said Marty.

A second shot.

Third.

Fourth.

"No..." Marshall shook his head. "No, they didn't. We just... we just talked about this! We weren't gonna have to kill any of them."

"Maybe someone tried to escape," Marty said.

"Fuck! Okay, let's get what we can, man. Grab the loot, grab the loot!" Marshall scooped as much as he could.

There was little left that Marty would have to grab. With the few hundreds he put in his sack, he also threw in that strange, interesting book.

He didn't know what it was about the play within the book. It just... it captivated him.

Marshall's eyes were bugging out, wide as saucers. "Fuck, man. Let's go!"

Soon, they tied their bags, flipped them over their shoulders, and rushed down to the bottom of the stairs.

The other four home invaders were waiting for them. The gunmen, Samson and Raymond, were looking at their feet, guns pointing downwards as well.

"You didn't," Marty said, looking at the gunmen. "You didn't kill the family."

"They could have told the cops anything," answered Samson.

"They didn't see our faces!" shouted Marshall.

"They know our heights," Raymond countered. "They know our voices, our frames. They could have seen our trucks outside."

"Fuck it," Marshall said. "Let's just get out of here."

The six men piled out of the house and towards their trucks. Throwing the loot in the back, they rolled out, back onto the country road.

***

Marty couldn't stop reading *The King in Yellow.*

After he and his six "friends" split the goods and money they found, each of them went on their merry little way. If they ever needed each other again for another robbery rendezvous, they were only phone calls away. For now, each of them got what they wanted, and were happy with their share.

Luckily, Marty already stashed the book in his sack, but he doubted any of the others would be into it, anyway. None of them were actors, or ever aspired to be. He doubted they even had an artistic bone in their body. They were all just desperate drug addicts, and found it easy to cooperate for their crimes. They would pull a few robberies here and there, in isolated country areas no one really cared about, make their money, and then enjoy their fixes until their payment ran out.

After smoking another round of ice in his run-down apartment, back in Sacramento, Marty's eyes read the words of *The King in Yellow* carefully, slowly, word by word. He worked to consume it, to feel it penetrate every ounce of his being, letting it run through his very body. He knew the characters by heart now. He knew the scenes, the world of Carcosa, the grand ball and the mask, the Stranger who evaded answering questions at every turn and corner. Such a strange, dark world, that environment of that dreadful play. What cryptic language the anonymous author used, what foul mannerisms some of the characters used to express themselves. And yet, as dark as that play was, everything was so extravagant, so opulent and beautiful.

Marty looked to the clock. 8:30, it said. But what day? And what time of day? Morning? Night? His blinds were drawn. He didn't know how long it'd been since he smoked his last round of ice, for time always ran like a bullet train whenever he smoked it. Existence didn't slow down for him, and before he knew it, Thursdays became Sundays, Sundays became Tuesday, and then, he would be broke again.

Such was the life for a meth-head.

Marty didn't dare to look in the mirror that was in his bedroom. No. He would stay in his bedroom, feel that euphoria rush through him, though it'd never feel as good as his first hit. To look in the mirror... the last time he did stare into the glass, even attempt to look at his face, all he could see were the scars, the wrinkles, the yellow and broken teeth, sunken eyes of a twenty-six year old man who appeared to be seventy-three. No, worse. Many an old man aged well, their teeth clean, their hair well-kept and skin shiny and rich. Marty remembered the pale complexion of a ghost in his features from the last time, and the soulless eyes of a dead man. That gorgeous actor, the one who stole girls' hearts up and down Hollywood Boulevard, the one who'd gain a part from a casting call based solely on his face, was gone now.

No. Marty wouldn't go into his bathroom. He'd stay in his dirty, filthy living room, surrounded by mess, lying on his couch as his high kept him going for hours and hours, his eyes rereading that book over, and over, and over again.

How many times had he read it? By now, he could imagine the long stretch of Lake Hali, the strange ghosts and ghouls that danced along its edges, the calling of spectral wolves as they hunted in the green. He could see the decrepit city streets of Carcosa, while the ruling class lost themselves in the ball, in the anticipation of dancing, singing, eating exquisite foods, laughing… and then the terror. The unveiling. The unveiling of the mask.

Marty looked at his clock again.

There was no time.

Literally, no time. No numbers on the clock.

"Fuck," Marty looked around, wondering if he'd lost power.

No. That flickering living room light was still kicking, weak, but with power. The lights in the kitchen were on, the mold and black stains on the wall more than visible.

Everything looked right, from what he could see.

The windows, concealed by blinds, still gave Marty no clue as to what time of day it was.

Curious, Marty rose from his seat after bookmarking *The King in Yellow* with his glass pipe. He stood and walked towards the window, drawing the blind.

Sickly yellow skies.

What a demented hue. The clouds, the air, everything out there looked like a swirl of apocalypse. Not a sun was in sight, but there were moons, not one, but two, giving some idea of night.

Two moons, both so magnified in the sky, bigger than the moon Marty was used to looking at, two spheres of rusty tones, ill-colored, one in insipid green and the other in corroded orange.

Marty was in awe. He knew he was high, under the spell of the crystal meth. The world outside his window, as fantastical as it appeared, seemed real. From the strange beasts that seemed to roam the tall, thick collections of dead grass around his apartment building, to the tormented birds that screeched high in those depressing skies, the dreamscape's authenticity was undeniable to Marty's eyes.

He didn't want that world to be real. He recognized it, the wilderness that surrounded that decrepit metropolis in the play.

The world of Carcosa.

"No." Marty shook his head, frowned, stepped back from the window. "No, man. This isn't real. This isn't fucking real."

Schizophrenia. This was an illusion, something Marty concocted in his mind. He was sure of it. Meth was known to bring about strange shifts of reality, and he suffered from hallucinations every now and then. None of them, however, had seemed as reality-altering as this moment.

This was on a whole different level of insanity. For the entire world to change, outside of his window, was more intense. No matter how many times he looked back to the window, blinked, and rubbed his eyes, the horrendous world of Carcosa remained, as if waiting for him to step out into its web.

Marty thought it safer to stay inside.

Then, the inside changed. It was a room, but not *his* room. Not *his* apartment.

He was back in that house.

Back in the house they robbed, just a week ago. Back in the country, further up north than Sacramento. He recognized its old furniture, the packed bookshelves.

God, that *room*. He was back in that den.

He turned to see the open safe. Within it was the book, the one with that squiggly, yellow sign.

The book glowed in that sickly color.

"What the fuck is going on?" Marty asked, as if someone could provide him with answers. He hoped they could, hoped they could give him some idea of what was going on.

Marty walked to the door of the den, and opened it.

Outside of the room, it was as if the rest of the house didn't exist. Carcosa stretched out around him, its long grass, and a putrid smell that made him want to throw up. A smell of death and decay, of pollution and blood. Past the tall grass, yards away, Marty could see demonic shapes, beasts unlike any he'd ever seen rummaging through the wild field.

Marty shut that door again, locked it, and pressed against it.

He wouldn't dare come out.

"Just gotta wait to come down," Marty said. "God, I'm quitting this shit. That's it. I'm going to rehab. I can't... damn ice... ruined my life."

Marty looked back to the window. The world was still there, still taunting his senses. None of it made any sense. Those snarling, wild beasts, making the most alien of howls and screeches that Marty ever heard, unlike any wolf, hyena, jackal, or other animal Marty could imagine. Looking at the two massive moons with their dull glow and dreadfully enlarged craters made Marty feel sick, as if they were magnets sucking away his vitality.

"This place isn't real," Marty said, repeating it like a sacred mantra. "This place isn't real. This place isn't real. This place-"

The King in Yellow play, still glowing in its sickly yellow, leaped from the safe and onto the center of the floor, in front of Marty. As Marty stared at the book, he saw the cover open as the book's pages flipped from left to right, as if by a magic wind. As the pages flipped, he could see the scenes of the play taking place in his mind... the stranger... Cassilda... the dance... the unmasking-

"Stop!" Marty yelled. "I don't want to see him! I don't want to see the King!"

Yes, the King. Marty remembered the descriptions from the book. The King in Yellow was who ruled this strange domain, covered in his tattered fabrics, grotesque face hidden from the world. When his face was unveiled, it evoked utter madness and chaos, ripping spectators from the inside out.

Marty glanced away from the book as it closed. His eyes sailed back to the window.

Out on the field, he could see familiar figures. There was Lou, Marshall, Samson, Raymond, Ben.

Marty's partners in crime. His fellow robbers. They were all wandering the fields, fear staining their zoned out eyes, their sunken meth faces possessed with so much dread, so much terror, lost in despair.

"Raymond!" Marty shouted, his back still pressed against the door, afraid to pull away. Who knew who would come in? Sure, the door was locked, but the door was wooden, and could be broken easily. "Lou! Marshall! Guys, I'm in here! Hurry, please!"

But the five were lost in their own little worlds, and they didn't seem to see Marty, much less each other. They were looking around, surprised to find themselves in such a distant, devilish location.

A beast leaped upon Lou, its large black claws sinking into his flesh as a bite slammed into his neck.

Raymond was tackled by those strange, extraterrestrial beasts as well. Ben screamed when monsters took him down, breaking his legs, snapping his arms.

Marty could hear everything. The screams as his five accomplices were grabbed by wild Carcosan demons, the clipping of limbs, the tearing of flesh. Marty's wide eyes couldn't look away, though he wished he could shut them, but they were held to those scenes of death as if by magnetism.

The power of the moons. Yes, that was it. They were holding him still and stiff against the door, his eyes frozen, widened like those terrible lunar forces. Nothing would stop them from watching, and his heart raced as he watched each of the five men reduced to flesh bits.

They weren't going to get him.

Marty would make sure of that. He raced to one of the book shelves, the one closest to the door. God, it was heavy, but a nice, persistent tilt finally sent the thing crashing to the floor. Books scattered as Marty pushed the base of the bookshelf, aligning it against the door as skillfully as he possibly could. Then, he looked around the room for other things, less heavy, to push against the door. There was a coffee table, thankfully, which Marty found effortless to push in front of the bookshelf. Then, he grabbed an ottoman threw it on top of the toppled bookshelf.

Safe. Marty was going to be safe.

He turned around, and his heart stopped. Where there were once the walls of that den, he found himself in another place entirely. Yes, the den of that country house in Northern California was gone, all gone. Where he was now was unfamiliar at first, then he realized he knew it all too well. He knew this location not from being there before, or even from seeing it in pictures, but from *text.*

The King in Yellow text. The play.

This was the palace of the King in Yellow. Ginormous stone with cracks built the walls of that melancholic castle. The rusty ebony gates that marked off forbidden rooms wore skulls atop some of its spikes. Various other fragments of bone rested on the stone floor as well.

Marty stepped back, his hands out in front of him.

Then, he bumped into something. *Someone.*

Marty turned.

A tall figure in tattered, moldy clothes greeted him. Tall was an understatement. The figure, draped in his pale yellow rags and shadows, wore a mask of the same bland color, his head extending nearly against the tall ceiling.

Shivering, Marty took a slow step back.

"Welcome, friend," said another voice.

Marty looked around to find four people he knew well, who he'd never forget. How he tried to forget their faces, every night that week, consuming as much crystal as he could to forget reality. Now, they were clear as day. There was the father, the mother, the daughter and the son, their faces expressionless, their skin mildewed in that tasteless yellow hue.

In an even brighter yellow, scribbled upon each of the family members' foreheads, was the squiggly yellow sign.

"We're so happy you could join us," the father said with his bland face. "Now, we can worship and serve him forever. He has placed his blessing upon us all. Aren't we lucky?"

Marty's face grew sullen, his wrinkled lips opening to reveal the last few teeth he owned. "I'm sorry. I didn't know they were going to kill you. It was an accident! We were just gonna take what we could take... grab whatever you had available."

"Oh, you have no need to apologize to us," the father said. "We're merely servants. Me. The wife. The children. And now, you."

Marty shook his head, shaking.

"You read the play, yes?" the mother asked.

Tears streamed down Marty's face. "I wish I didn't. Wish I never touched the thing."

"It found you," the mother said. "Just like it did nearly a century ago, when people found it again. It touched them, and changed things. But the government tried to suppress it, tried to pretend the play didn't even exist."

"We found a copy," said the daughter. She pointed to her brother. "Me and Terry here, when we were playing in the woods."

"We searched the interwebs," said the father. "Learned all about it. About its power. About why it's feared. About our beloved King."

"And now, you know him, too," said the son with a gap-toothed smile.

"I don't want to know him," Marty said, his spaced-out eyes suddenly brought down to Earth, held in a space he didn't want to be in. "I don't want to be here, or have anything to do with this!"

"You don't have a choice," the father said. "The book found you, after it found us. It chose you, just as it chose us. Just as you chose us."

"Please, let me go." Marty fell to his knees, folded his hands with clasping fingers. "I swear, I'll change. I'll go to rehab. I'll stop smoking. Stop stealing from people, stop everything bad I'm doing."

"But what you did was good!" the father shouted. "It brought you to us! It brought you here!"

"And then you liberated us!" said mother. "For weeks, we were tortured with all of those dreams of Carcosa, of the sign, of the wild animals and this uncanny city. We were so afraid."

"Then, you killed us," said the father. "You liberated us, and now we are under his blessing."

Marty didn't want to turn back around, didn't want to see the king again.

"You must die for liberation," said the mother.

Each of the family members reached into their clothing and pulled out long, sharp knives.

Marty gazed upon them with terror. "Please, don't!"

"The sooner you die," said the father, "the sooner you can see the King."

"And then, you will be reborn," promised the son as he moved in with his knife, accompanied by his family.

With more feeble attempts at protests and promises, Marty cried out to the family, but they refused to listen to another word. The first knife descended, then the second, and the third. Soon, each of the four knives repeated in their downwards stabbing, sinking into Marty's flesh as he shrieked, feeling agonizing pain. The blood squirted and dripped down Marty's flesh, down the faces of the family and down their clothes. Each punctured wound rewarded the blades with more hot red, and they couldn't get enough, tearing into the flesh for more.

Marty's screams pleased the King standing behind him. The family could feel the King's approval, and rested assured that Marty's fatal torture would be awarded once his forehead was anointed with that yellow sign.

Venusian Hell

Beyond the black, Babylonian sky, the necropolis of Carcosa calls him again. The tatters of The King fold and unfold in his mind, and he waits, listening to the dark utterances of his decadent servants.

Overlooking the stars of Taurus on his chart once again, his fingers trail each section of that deadly constellation. From Hastur to Aldebaran, from the Pleiades to Algol, he can feel the King's presence. Those gothic calls cannot be denied, cannot be ignored.

By now, Adamen Gizzal the Mage has seen many of his peers die in their secret work. Where they once scoured the cosmos in deep thought and meditation after rituals to connect to their gods and goddesses, the powerful deities that preserved and helped their people through the mysteries of the elements, they found a detour. The King was intoxicating and distracting in his radiating passion, that dim golden light that burned in the eye of the Tauran constellation, the same constellation Adamen and his peers called Gugalanna, The Bull of Heaven. He coaxed them with his fluttering robe extensions, showed them a world beyond their wildest imaginations, wowed and frightened them all at the same time.

Then, they fell like lotuses, one after the other. The King would require tasks of his new enslaved acolytes, worship ceremonies, deeds to be done. When he was done with one of them, they were done. Bones cracked in the grip of invisible forces, mouths vomited with blood and organ contents, bodies broken under random human stampedes in the Babylonian streets as denizens were struck with divine frenzy. Magician after magician, mystic after mystic, all entering that dark, abysmal kingdom.

Forced to focus upon The Bull of Heaven again in his quiet, isolated chambers, Adamen calls to his gods and goddesses- Enki, Ishtar, Murduk- may they all preserve him in this strange quest he's been tricked into. Especially Ishtar, Goddess of Love and Fertility, the feminine force that *understands the properties of Venus, inside and out. May she protect him from the planet's harsh attributes, from its correlating constellation of Taurus with its harsh aspects.*

    But he knows too late. After years of soul travels, lured by the waters of Lake Hali and the forever decaying, decadent city of Carcosa, its demonic inhabitants and dark wonders, The King's tatters have him in their clutches. Though he cannot always see them, those sick yellow strands of deathly silk, he can always feel them, and like an insect in webs he waits for the moment The King shall swallow him whole.

    Not yet. The King has more in store for him. Adamen Gizzal the Mage must write. If he does not, he shall feel The King's royal, divine wrath, and be consumed by the golden flames of his malevolent servants.

    Those words he puts on parchment fill him to the blood with dread and fear. They are words of pain, hate, and torture hidden behind sweet, affected language. A play, with acts, characters, props and dreams unveiling some deeply hidden, cosmic, venereal hell, where things like love, sex, desire, and longing unveil more wickedness, more torture, more destruction.

A play that forms a book, lengthy and powerful with each word. A book that reveals a holy, dark force, which has craved the world since its inception.

The book must be opened. Again, then again, age after age.

And blood will spill. Pain will endure, everlasting, forever and ever.

*

Alicia Meadows couldn't stop thinking about the markings they found on that strange exoplanet, now named Morgan.

As an astronaut in the American Space Program, Alicia never thought that mankind would ever find evidence of a possibly humanoid, intelligent species in the cosmos, at least not in her lifetime. Now, Alicia and the seven crew members she traveled with aboard the Blackburn 150X had made history accomplishing such a feat. Five years before, in late April of 2011, she and her team had found wreckage of extraterrestrial spacecraft on a foreign, lonely planet outside of their Solar System. All over the hard shelled vehicles were a strange, pale yellow, squiggly marking. When the astronauts brought samples of the debris back, ASP sent the recovered fragments to labs, had them analyzed, and even did a segment of their findings on international news.

ASP soon regretted their decision to make the discoveries public. Days and weeks after the footage of the debris and their curious markings were broadcast on the news, a number of reports broke out of people in maniacal states, committing suicide, homicides, and genocides in different pockets of the world. Cults drank poisons, artists stabbed teachers in illustration studios and classes, intellectuals writhed in psychotic states at conferences and seminars. In all of these cases, that strange sign was present, those pale yellow squiggly lines appearing in photographs throughout the press.

What was the deal with that strange, urine tinted pictorial scrawling, Alicia had wondered for months. She had searched the DigiWebs, hoping to find information on that sign, but data was hard to find. Even online records of the earlier news broadcast showing off the findings of the Blackburn 150X expedition were next to nil. Though one or two typed articles discussed the interesting wreckage as signs of extraterrestrial life, none of the articles even spoke of the same scrawlings found on the shattered vehicle shards, and there were no pictures.

When Alicia tried to get records from ASP, her requests were denied. Her attempts to speak about the strange yellow scribble with her colleagues, supervisors, ASP scientists and managers were met with scowls and derailing language. *We should have never shared that information with the public* was along the lines of what many of the higher-ups at ASP were saying. *Discuss the wreckage with no one. We're still doing analysis on the artifacts. Concentrate on your job and do your work.*

As the months dragged, Alicia's work had consisted of tracking the progress of probes and testing equipment for other astronauts. She doubted she'd be on call for another expedition anytime soon. All the while, a number of crew members from the Blackburn 150X were dying. First, there was

Raj Chatterjee, who had acquired a mysterious fever three months after the flight. Medical officials said he was showing flu-like symptoms that first week of sickness, but after three weeks, Raj had been in a hospital, comatose and strapped to wires for nourishment. He died before the doctors could make heads or tails of what horrid disease had invaded his body, confused by the lack of viral signs his body and fluids showed in testing.

Nathan Ianni was next. Months later, he had been struck with blindness, his kidneys failing. He died a short period after. Sarah Donahue was struck by a crumbling statue in a museum, her head caved in by heavy stone. By Erin Tracey's death, less than a year after the expedition, Ashley was just waiting to die. She knew it had something to do with those discoveries, that strange space debris they found and brought back. Ashley tried to communicate with the others, see if they had any idea of what was going on, but everyone was tight lipped if they *did* know. Gregory Baker swore he had no clue why other members of the crew were dying, and then he died a week later of a heart attack in his living room.

The funeral home is just around the corner, Ashley would think, constantly, trying to get lost in her work, to forget what they found, but she couldn't. The thoughts plagued her day after day, brought agony to her tired mind. Sleepless nights were spent lying in the dark, hoping that her end would wait another day. At least until she had some clues, some answers.

And the clues came. After the seventh death, when Ashley was the last one of the crew left.

A few more expeditions with other crews had been made to the exoplanet, Morgan, and more wreckage was brought back for analysis. Obviously, ASP was still interested in the material, though they were tight-lipped about it. In her free time, away from work, Ashley was still searching the DigiWebs, typing in "Yellow Scribbles" and "Extraterrestrials", keyword after keyword that would bring back the same websites and articles, the same conspiracy theories that were so loopy that no shred of reliable evidence could be gathered from them.

After nearly two years of perusing, she found something that gave her interest.

The Yellow Sign. And there were pictures, scrawlings from a century or more ago, showing that same weird symbol. Drawn on papers, on the sides of buildings and floors, carved in tables and columns, the sign had been seen in many places.

Ashley wanted to know what the sign was about. What could it mean, what did it represent? Searching through what she could find, she found out about an old play that had been written, once widespread throughout the United States and the world: *The King in Yellow.*

The surface of the book had that weird, yellow sign. It had been banned from the public decades ago, over half a century, and book burnings had been held all over the world for it. People swore up and down that the book was evil, a demonic remnant of an old, forgotten and superstitious world. The book was purported to drive men and women crazy, to push them to make dreadful choices and do horrible things.

The book was a play. No one knew the original author, where the book came from or when it first came into existence. There were rumors that the play was written in other languages before its English translation, editions spanning from Arabic to Latin. The earliest documented use of the play was in Elizabethan England, when a newly formed theatrical company toured the English countryside, acting out *The King in Yellow* for many a spectator from Brighton to York. When word spread of audience members breaking out in frenzies, killing each other or dying from sickness days later, The Queen ordered the play banned and the actors hanged. Curiously, all actors that had performed in the play were found dead before they could be executed, often under extreme circumstances. One report said a young crossdresser that played a female part named *Camilla* in the play was found with butchered eye sockets and dangling entrails in a Lancashire barn. Another actor, who played the part of The King in Yellow himself, was rumored to be burnt to a crisp inside of a Bath bathhouse.

Alicia didn't know how much of these ridiculous stories she could believe, but they were very interesting, and they *did* connect to The Yellow Sign. She researched everything she could about *The King in Yellow*. There was never anything positive to say about the play. All history of it linked to death, despair, and destruction. Every link on the DigiWeb swore that the book had been eradicated forever, that there were no other copies, and that even if a copy did exist, anyone caught with the book could face serious consequences under law.

Could a play really be that bad? Besides, she doubted anyone could really ensure that all of the books had been destroyed. Some people out there must have kept copies, collectors, anti-censorship freaks, and protectors of the words who believed in literary preservation. If *The King In Yellow* was really so emotionally provoking, so captivating of a work to possibly cause death by strange, arcane circumstances, then the curiosity of man would always keep it alive.

Curiosity brewed in Alicia's own heart, binding her mind with a weird, queer feeling. She wanted to know the work of *The King in Yellow* for herself. Up close and personal, the words for her to read and figure out beyond hearsay and fearful, deluded beliefs. What was that play *really* about?

She had found different characters from the play here and there on old websites- Camilla, The Stranger, The King in Yellow, Cassilda. There was a weird prop called The Pallid Mask, worn by The Stranger, though some sites proclaimed the mask wasn't a real mask, but The King's real face. Records of plays performed in the past swore that the actors portraying The Stranger never actually wore a mask, but their faces literally changed in the course of the play, seemingly possessed with a deathly yellow glow akin to the color of The Yellow Sign.

On her days and evenings off, obsessed with the possibility that the play could exist somewhere on the DigiWebs, Alicia searched hard for a digital document. Every day, she seemed to find the same snippets, the same lines and images of The Yellow Sign. To no avail could she find the real play on her own.

One evening, while checking her messages, Alicia came upon an interesting note from a stranger. He introduced himself as Karl Bennett, and stated that he had made the acquaintance of the other members in Alicia's old Blackburn 150X crew. All of them had been interested in The Yellow Sign after their "exposure" to the symbol on Morgan, and Karl had been most curious about the crew after seeing the news broadcast. He said he had been an avid devotee of The King since he had read the play over a decade before, finding it in one of his many hacking escapades among many other books banned by the government. Knowing The Yellow Sign like the back of his hand, news of space wreckage found with the symbol had peaked his interest. Karl had become obsessed with the Blackburn 150X expedition, and he had studied up all he could find about the crew members in the ASP database. He took his time to contact them all when his King had stated the time was right, one by one, and given them the play they had so desperately heard about online. All they had to do was read it, front to back, in its entirety.

I am merely a servant of His Grace in Carcosa, Karl proclaimed, *nothing more.*

When you found that spacecraft debris and became witnesses to The Yellow Sign that embodies the living spirit of Carcosa in the eye of Taurus, you became servants as well. The others have done their part. Now, your time has come.

Attached to the document was a full length file of *The King in Yellow*.

*

By the time Alicia was done reading the play, she felt no regrets.

The curiosity wasn't necessarily gone. Though she knew the characters now, the scenes, the lines and acts, there were still some queries that plagued her mind. How could such a play inspire such madness, drive people so easily from reason and logic, inspire them to do the most treacherous things? Sure, she had felt a powerful spirit of dread and terror in each and every word she had read, seen horror within each character of that play, personas she even believed to merely represent different aspects of The King Himself, of His haunted kingdom Carcosa and the melancholy Lake Hali that surrounded it. Alicia knew the play was capable of evoking such wild, dangerous emotions within a human being, but *how?* What was The King's magical ability to cause such reactions in people, if He truly did exist?

There was a passion in each line, each sentence, that knitted like some unbreakable, impenetrable ethereal force. Once caught, one couldn't turn away or break away, and the power of The King was crippling, maddening, intoxicating.

*

Alicia began to have horrendous nightmares.

She dreamed of alien cultures, spread throughout the cosmos, all looking towards that bull constellation. Scribes and seers amongst their tribes and nations communicated with those stars, evoked golden spectral ambassadors from Carcosa with their magical rituals that showed them away. Eventually, swayed by the ambassador's promises to preserve and empower their peoples, the scribes were lost in their charms. Their words brought great pain to their people, and civilizations died out, flesh rotting, body parts distorted, faces burned in the awakening of The Pallid Mask.

She dreamed of extraterrestrial armies and sojourners lost in the sway of The Yellow Sign ages ago, scouring the cosmos to spread their wicked gospels. They would destroy other foreign alien planets and cultures to eventually destroy their own, The Yellow Sign being the only thing that ever endured once their kinds fell.

Over and over again, as if caught in a bad domino effect of karma, Alicia saw the same scene play throughout the universe - different beings lost in the dread and chaos of that astral bull, corrupting and destroying all things around them. Many a Venus in many a star system correlated to the beat of that Taurus constellation, reflecting its unending desire, its undying love for death and desolation.

She dreamed of human beings throughout the history of her planet, looking up at that lovely morning star, Venus, the intoxicating planet, and enraptured with Taurus, the very constellation they believed to be ruled by the planet of love. They built temples, wrote poems, gave their lives in dedication to goddesses symbolizing that heavenly body. Alicia could see as some of those mystics and devotees wishing to probe the mysteries behind the planet and its correlating constellation soon fell upon the brightly burning Taurean eye of Aldebaran. Lost in its sway, traveling by the soul, they came upon the mysterious black city of Carcosa, lost forever. Many died, lost in its devilish grip, all after committing the tasks they were sworn to uphold.

She saw the writing of the book. She could smell the incense burning in its production, and she saw a language scribbled that was completely foreign to her, completely beyond her grasp as she looked down to a brown hand.

She dreamed she was Raj Chatterjee, participating in disgusting orgies with prostitutes in motel rooms after his day shifts, bludgeoning them for sacrifices to an invisible, yellow god that held him captive in silky webs. Nathan Ianni followed art students and models home after college courses, stabbing them to death in alleys before chanting over their bodies in a weird, cryptic tongue he only described as

"Carcosan". Erin Tracey went on hunts in nightclubs after hours, seducing men and murdering them in their vehicles after rendezvouses in countryside make out spots. Paul, Whitney, all of her former crewmates, had spilled blood for their king, their god-

And now it was her turn.

Waking up in cold sweat, breathing profusely, Alicia wanted to ignore her fate, her duty. She wanted to break away from those coils that she had once felt holding her, pulling her like a lantern in the depths of the universe surrounding her, but she couldn't break away. No matter how much she wished to be independent and free, she was trapped now. The King had her, and she would worship. She would obey.

Falling on her knees, prostrating in the darkness, her body faced the constellation of Taurus. Even in the pitch black room, illuminated only by the red numbers on her digital alarm clock, Alicia knew where The Bull of Heaven rested overhead. She would listen and obey, doing what needed to be done.

*

A legacy was behind her.

Alicia knew that now. She had quit her job at ASP. There was nothing left for her there. The others had fulfilled their missions. Now, she would do the same until The King granted her liberation through her own cherished death.

Hitchhiking through the country, Alicia meditated on the words of the play constantly, from sunrise to sunset. As she chatted with her drivers, sharing details of her past as an astronaut, she thought of those lines, those characters, each prop and location outlined in that accursed play. Moving through those lonely interstate roads, she could see the brilliance of each scene, how they had to be performed just right, just perfectly aligned to each and every star in that heavenly constellation. She knew it well now, from her studies of ancient astrology, mixed with her astronomical education. She understood the will and natures of The Pleiades, those weeping sisters, and Algol, that ghoul's head, the stars of Hastur and the Hyades. She knew how they all bowed to Aldebaran, that brilliantly foul eye that housed black Carcosa, kingdom of The King in Yellow.

At the end of every ride, congratulating each kind Samaritan with the hammer concealed properly in her handbag, Alicia focused upon her King with great intention. She murmured the words of Carcosan that sailed from her throat with accurate pronunciation, coldly staring at her victims as she pummeled their brains in. Each word was stated perfectly, each action carried through with reverence and modesty.

Each sacrifice would bring The King's dream closer to her primitive planet. His well-deserved terrestrial expansion, The Imperial Dynasty of America, would be realized on Earth, and all would bend their knees for his arrival.

But Alicia would not take any credit when His dream came into fruition. She was merely a servant, doing The King's great work as many had done before her and would do after her.

Aldebaran Apocalypse

It had always been considered an unlucky star, set in the stubborn and wanton, perhaps even daemonic, constellation of Taurus. Aldebaran, the bold bull's eye and home of the King in Yellow, lorded over the forever tragic and depressed Pleiades. As a hateful sun, it gazed upon its planets with anger and want, always craving for dominance, lusting to conquer, to destroy...

The world had known to fear that star, though they didn't know why. Always proving an unfavorable aspect, a source of decapitations, sorrow, and murder, the seers of many a culture forever feared the fates of Aldebaran. ***Al Dabaran,*** *the follower as named by the ancient Muslim astrologers, was seen to trail behind the Hyades as if it had a relentless death wish, enslaved to* its own desires. To the Hindu astrologers, it was Rohini, the red one, a double-edged source of romance and destruction, its seemingly auspicious charms of superficial love wed with violent death. To the Romans, it was Palilcium, a symbol of flocks and followers, of meek sheep and loyal lambs.

Only the foolish would worship such a star. Only the weak would give into its charms, to celebrate it as they did in the Roman days of the Parilian festivals. Like the maenads who slaughtered for their bull god during the Bacchanalia, those under the sway of Aldebaran would bring chaos and destruction under its command.

Yet the enslaved did not see their ruler until He revealed his face to them... if He so chose. The King who had forever imposed His might from the city of Carcosa, which sat upon the chief planet that orbited the passionate star of Aldebaran, ensured that all of His subjects acted out His whims and did as He told them to do. If not, they would meet their fatal end, if not by His hand then by his own ravenous denizens. The Carcosans had followed His commands for eons, pillaging and murdering from one planet to another.

Now, Earth would be under His rule. The very distant planet that had feared Him for thousands of years, where astrologers and mediums had often entered frenzy and screamed upon entering His presence, many committing suicide afterwards. The planet that had often captured His imagination, amused Him with how feeble and primitive its people were. Even the most skeptical of them, the ones who didn't believe in the influence of the stars, were ruled by the cosmos so easily from their attitudes and personalities to their very actions, fates *acted out perfectly from the day they were born.*

But the day had come, the glorious date when all upon that decrepit globe would fall under the sway of one fate and one fate only- supreme death at the hands of The King in Yellow. He would bring destruction with pride, allowing His pallid light to shine from the red eye of His perfect star... and let them slaughter each other one by one, His perfect, pretty sheep, to remodel their world like His own.

*

400 BCE, Southwest Anatolia

Chara displayed The Sign of the Yellow- her right index finger curled to her lip as her left hand did a sweeping motion against her neck- before two tall bronze-skinned guards at the front of the secluded cave.

"My life to sacrifice in silence," Chara said, her limited Carian accented with native Greek pronunciation. "His glory to gain."

She'd been taught the sign by her brother, Diogenes, as well as the introductory phrases and etiquette. Diogenes, a member of this mystery cult, now vouched as her witness to initation. Family ties, however, would not guarantee that Chara would be initiated tonight- only He would decide if she were worthy.

After Chara's inhaled the burning branches of purifying herbs that wafted over her dirty dress, she was sprinkled with holy water. Her brother softly marked her head with a smear of yellow paste, then lifted his torch and led the way. Chara followed him into the cave.

"The world, you leave behind you," said Diogenes in their native Greek, "enshrouded by night and ignorance. May His pallid light revive you with knowledge and wisdom."

A woman in the pale-yellow mask greeted Diogenes and Chara not too far from the entrance. Upon her forehead was The Yellow Sign, golden in its snakelike hooks and enigmatic curls. A magnetic pull seemed to emanate from that symbol; though Diogenes had shown Chara the sign many times in the past year, it was different seeing it now. Sure, the sign has enticed Chara before and made her curious about her brother's secret religion, but this feeling was more than fascination. Some vacuum, some force, drew her spirit towards the sign with an unavoidable presence.

The brother spoke to the woman in Carian. Diogenes had only taught Chara a few phrases and words from the language so far, and none of the vocabulary she had learned accompanied this current exchange. Diogenes promised to teach her more in time, as she learned the ways of The

King, how to worship Him and even perform His magic if He deemed her a worthy sorcercess.

The Carian woman in the mask looked to Chara. "Are you prepared, child of beasts? Do you believe yourself worthy of The King's high knowledge and blessings?"

"I do." Chara presented a courageous face, at least she hoped she did, as the masked woman's sierra eyes emitted the same magnetic energy as the sign on her forehead. "I've studied all His Grace would allow me to see... through the mercy of His agent Hound, my brother and witness. Hound provided me with the apocalyptic prophecies of His Grace, through the lessons and the mystery play that should never be confined to the written word. I believe in His sovereignty. I wish to serve Him in mystery and magic."

The masked woman looked to Diogenes. "She learned the initiate lines well, Brother Hound. You stumbled over yours when your father brought you in. No mere dog like yourself, eh?"

Chara bit her lip, hoping the Carian woman did not see that quick reaction. Chara knew her father failed the cult, which led to his execution. Being privy to such knowledge wasn't easy, nor did it comfort her to see brother's chastisement, but she couldn't allow such things to shake her confidence. Her heart still ached when her brother told her how he'd been knocked down a rank and moved from the cult's inner order to the less esteemed outer order, cruelly renamed from Brother Bullseye to Brother Dog. He'd been told that he needed to make up for the sins of his father in order to gain honor once again. Now, he offered his sister for initiation, which would gain him some redeeming quality. Two could make up for a betrayer better than one as they served The Great Work of the cult, especially when combined with the work her brother and father had done before the betrayal. Diogenes hadn't been exiled; he'd been reprimanded. There were many chances for him to rejoin to the inner order of the cult, hopefully with his sister right behind him. Their father had done what he'd done, but they would show them. Diogenes would be nothing like her father. *She* would be nothing like her father.

We do not hold the same privileges here as foreigners that we possess at home, Chara reminded herself. *Grecians in another land, another territory, in a secret group hidden from even their own population. In our fatherland, we are wealthy nobles shielded from the plights of commoners. Here, we are the spawn of a traitor. I will prove myself. I will hold my tongue. I will not reveal the secrets.*

The play must remain in the dark, never committed to paper, never shared with outsiders.

After her long and tense scolding of Diogenes, the masked woman leaned towards Chara with a bold gaze. "The concealing of the sacred lessons and the sacred play," she said in Carian-accented yet fluent Greek. "Of the apocalypse. That none of it will never grace papyri. Are you a believer and will you uphold the laws?"

"I know the prophecy of the ultimate traitor, if that's what you're asking," said Chara. "I know that someone will violate the code of honor and release the secrets to the swine of the night. That The King's word will penetrate the masses who were never intended to understand it. As all reevaluations that flow from The King, I believe it to be true, but I doubt we will see such a travesty in our lifetimes, or our children in theirs, or our children's children."

"Most of the cult would say your father put the wheel in motion for that travesty," the masked woman said. "Perhaps he was the ultimate traitor. Perhaps the time is not only near, but *here.*"

"We are not my father," spat Chara, "and he failed in his betrayal. But he is not *the* betrayer. The King said that one shall remain anonymous even to us all, most likely because this cult of mystery will be long gone by the time we are betrayed."

"You know all of the pleasing notes to sing for His favor, don't you?" the masked woman asked. "As if you were born as an oracle of The Sign itself. Perhaps. Your natal chart did show a strong alignment to The King, even moreso than your brother or father." She took Diogenes' torch. "Let's go. We will see if you have the privilege of calling me sister later, child of beasts.

If you are worthy to be baptized by stardust or annihilated by it."

Chara's heart raced as she followed the Carian with her brother by her side. Diogenes had told her months ago that he would not be able to offer a comforting word or gesture if she chose to come to the cave for initiation, but he didn't have to whisper a word. She could feel his support, his *fear* for her, wondering if she would survive. He'd seen many die in these rituals, she knew; the lack of numbers in their confidential religion came from more than just exclusivity. Many *failed* to join. A decade into this cult, Diogenes knew the dangers. Father had only died three years ago; Chara had only learned the truth behind his end last week.

Do you still want to join? Diogenes had asked.

Yes. Father had served The King in Yellow for what- thirty years? Forty? And their grandfather, said to be the first Grecian allowed into this cult, had maintained their secrets until his natural death. She could do it. Chara could remain loyal. She would not share hidden things with peasants, would not present the gestures or lines of the play to outsiders. Heaven forbid that she ever even draw a slither of The Sign, not an arm nor a leg, not its central dot in public. Every aspect of the cult had to remain obscure. Protected. Out of reach from the mentally and spiritually destitute. The Yellow Sign and its King were only for His devotees.

How deep was that cave? The path moved downwards, sloped, with rocks breaking loose to roll away from their sandals. It felt as if they were entering the terrain of the underworld itself. Chara's legs, already tired from the long journey to Caria, throbbed with each step. She felt a bit disoriented, though she had drank water just an hour before, and it was a miracle that she had presented the initiate's declaration as clearly as she could. But it would all pay off soon, wouldn't it? Like her brother, she would gain access to the mark on her back, which would spread out and curl from the center of her spine. It would rest beneath her dress, taunting the world of men, of *beasts,* undignified and unkempt, savage plebeians too unsophisticated to wine and dine in Carcosa.

They reached a destination. Finally. There was an open hall down here with torches along the walls. Men and women, no more than thirty in total, wore pallid masks over the upper halves of their visages, their mouths free for slaughtered meat, dates, and wine. They exchanged conversation and laughter amongst themselves. The King's golden symbol shined upon their masks' foreheads.

"You may dance with us after His Grace deems you ready," their guide, still nameless, said as she looked to Chara. "And if you fail, then we bid you farewell as the dance continues without you." She looked to Diogenes. "And all must dance for Him, in life and in death."

"She'll make it," Diogenes snapped. He looked to Chara with shimmering wet eyes, his lips twitching. "Remember what I told you. Invoke His sign in His presence. In your mind. Stand strong."

"Surely you did not prime her more than that," said the masked woman. "That would be against the rules. It would spell your doom *and* hers. Just like your father. And if you did violate boundaries, He'll know. He always knows."

"He knows I did not and would not do such a thing," Diogenes said. "I gave the prerequisite lessons and instructions. My father violated the code. I did not. She won't."

The masked woman spat something out in her Carian tongue. Curses, no doubt, with the harsh tones behind those words. Once she'd gotten them out, she composed herself, and looked back to Chara as she took her hand. "Will you be my sister or will you fail?" she asked in a switch back to Greek. "We see now." She looked back to Diogenes. "Enjoy yourself."

The masked woman walked away from Diogenes as she held Chara's hand. Chara gave her brother one more curious look, capturing his sorrow and worry. Her heartbeat had slowed a bit; courage had been invoked, and the sign was strong in her consciousness. Though new to this environment, she would remain firm in this test. She had faith in her *gnosis,* her inner knowledge of The King, though limited. She had received the dreams she was supposed to get- the bull with the bright eyes that went from red to yellow hues, The Yellow Sign on the face of the moon and the waters of the Earth, the streets of the corroding city that was supposed to be Carcosa. He would know that she got His messages. He had already deemed her ready.

Out of the hall, down another descending corridor, then one slightly ascending, another even-leveled, another... the merry chortles and clanks of gauntlets had long faded behind Chara and her escort. The torch granted little illumination in this vast chthonic labyrinth, and the masked woman offered no warm comforts of a companion... at least not yet.

They finally reached an end. A jagged wall stood in front of them. Long spikes hung overhead, probably as old as the cave itself; Chara imagined the one above her breaking off and stabbing her skull on impact.

What a cruel punishment from The King that would be, Chara thought. *A proper sacrifice in exchange for the sins of my father, cleansing my brother and the cult once more. I would accept such a fate if he refused me as a devotee.*

"So what's here?" Chara asked as she freed her hand from the cold escort's grasp, tired of the silence. "The test. I'm ready."

The masked woman looked into Chara's eyes, her own sierra orbs enflamed. "I like your emotion. Your heart. Reminds me of myself, though it took me years to develop long after my initiation. You're stronger than Diogenes." The woman pointed to the ceiling. "He awaits there. Stand here. He'll come to you soon. He will know if you are worthy or not." The masked woman turned and walked towards the corridor's exit with torch in hand.

"Wait!" Chara called behind her. "What will I call you, sister? If I make it through the night."

The masked woman chuckled. "You will know me as Cassilda, child of beasts... until His Grace deems otherwise."

Chara watched the woman disappear behind the turn of the corridor, the flicker of the torch growing faint so quickly. Darkness fell. Chara's heart raced again and she looked back up at the ceiling. Being unable to see the sharp stalactites, to see *anything,* that mocked her from above only fed an ignited anxiety. She hoped that her patience would soon be rewarded.

Cassilda, Chara thought. *An important character in the play, second to only The King. What a heartless jest. I truly wish to know her name... to know her as a sister. I feel she would be kind to me once she saw my work. That we would be friends. I must pass. I... I will pass.*

Chara saw something.

A star. Then two. Then four. The entire constellation of Taurus presented itself within seconds, astral spheres bright in their formation. More segments of the night sky revealed themselves overtime, though Taurus stood pronounced, popping out at Chara with a stubborn, furious energy to its composition. The orb of Aldebaran soon flamed red, the most demanding star of them all.

The Bull of Heaven, Chara recognized. She studied every star of it since her brother had given her the primary lessons, the only information he could share with her before joining the mystery cult of The King in Yellow. She knew the tragic and melancholic Pleiades. She knew the gorgon star of Algol, mad and furious, Medusa's decapitated head of misery.

She knew Aldebaran, ruler of the bull, home of The King's holy Carcosa-

The Sign remained strong in Chara's mind. She clung to it, her only saving grace, as emotions of dread washed over her with terror instilled in her heart. She recited the Carcosan prayer her brother gave her, hoped it would grant her mercy. *The city falls under His sway, the light strong in its pale illumination, His star enlivened with holy rage-*

Aldebaran shined brighter and grew larger as the cosmos around it shrank. Its redness turned an even more unsettling yellow, drained and lifeless, sucking at the air around it with a parasitic fashion. Spheres of various colors spun around the dirty star. *Other worlds,* as her brother had told her, *and our own is not as flat as the astronomy of outsiders say. Diogenes said we rotate around our sun like that, along with Venus, Mercury, and the other planets.* One sphere enlarged beyond the others- the home of Carcosa, as Chara knew- and it wasn't long before dead seas filled with carrion swam into view, terrains with grey and black grass stretched with disease. Then, The King's city spread out before her. Carcosa, just like Chara's dream, with its uneven, lonely streets, ebony spires, and corroded towers. Carcosa, a city of death, a capital of fear, chaos and destruction, just as its King desired. She could smell the decay and decrepit bodies, the stench of eternal death.

The courtyard awaited. The gates parted.

Chara's chest ached. Tears poured from her eyes. The uncompromising pull of these sights did not allow her to look down or away.

But I am strong. I wanted this. Why would I look away?

Her vision ascended cold black steps. They entered a dark, wretched castle adorned with pallid walls. Dead wraiths, felt but not seen, screamed in agony.

This pleases The King, she knew.

In his throne room, he appeared. He was nothing like she thought he would be. He was everything, and yet...

Chara held her ground, though she wanted to crumble to her knees. She mouthed the crucial lines of the play, though she wished she didn't have to remember them. She played Cassilda well, and knew she did from the violent yet amused look in his eyes, but the whole time she wished she was someone else. Not Chara, not Cassilda, not one of His chosen.

Hot sensations rippled deep along Chara's back. She smelled the burning of her skin, her clothes. She screamed as the forming marks cut deep. Fire burned through the fabric of her dress and blood dripped down her skin as bruises formed. Her wide eyes continued to look upwards, enthralled by The King who stared back at her.

In her pain, her *praise,* and his joy, all else fell silent.

*

21st Century, America

Robbie's breakfast hit the spot-buttered toast with eggs and a glass of orange juice.

While he savored his meal before a long day, Robbie watched the news. No shocker came when the headline story revolved around the American Space Program and its struggle to understand the alien artifacts they were finding, along with the hieroglyphs they couldn't decode. The ASP had become a major feature in the news for the past half a decade, as more hacked documents leaked about their discoveries of exoplanets and ancient extraterrestrial spacecraft. Such a mess would be easier for the ASP to clean up if so many deaths hadn't accompanied their operations, and if they could gain a clue on what was behind all of the chaos. From the two astronauts slaughtered on an exoplanet years ago to the explosion of a space center that housed some of the discovered artifacts on other planets, the casualties of many other unfortunate and bizarre events filled the last few decades.

Robbie could only laugh at the farce of it all. The Digi-Webs and independent publications provided answers about these aliens, but major news sources didn't want to take those open forums seriously. Surely, an extraterrestrial monarch known to a select few on Earth throughout the millennia couldn't be real. It was all half-cooked tinfoil conspiracy theories, just wacky Georgie Tsekrekos fantasies as akin to The Mystery Channel 'documentaries', comedic to common sense, bane to pragmatism, and meme-worthy. An ancient celestial monarchy that still reigned within its star system across the galaxy came off the pages of science-fiction. No one with a respectable job or income, who didn't live in their mother's basement or collect Jokemon cards as adults, wanted to believe that a play laid at the center of extraterrestrial mystery.

Mystery. The perfect word for the charade, this King in Yellow business that was right out in the open, as the best mysteries always were. Who would have known that Robbie's interest in the mystery would occur just five years ago, when this business became more common to see in the news, and those dreams with the beautiful woman began.

Robbie yawned as he looked at his dissertation on his laptop. Just a few pages needed to be completed, then another read through, perhaps his... fifteenth? Sixteenth? He lost track. He'd changed so many of the pages over and over again, paragraph by paragraph, line by line, word by word throughout those three years. But now, he knew this would be a document that would make him earn his PHD with pride. The painstaking research, piles of books borrowed from a multitude of libraries, interviews conducted with experts throughout the scientific, philosophical, and archaeological fields. Oh yes. He earned this degree. This dissertation would change the world, hopefully before it was too late.

Robbie reread his dissertation's title again. *The Yellow Mystery Cult of the Carians and their Deity of Destruction Embodied as The King in Yellow.* Perfect. He didn't care if Professor Higgins said the title was too long; many dissertation titles were long as fuck! He didn't care if Professor Calhoun called it pretentious when she erroneously thought Robbie was making a Beatles reference, though it made him thankful he didn't have such a lame sense of humor. The title captured what the dissertation was about. One look at the title was all anyone needed to see that Robbie found links between The King in Yellow play and an ancient Anatolian cult.

Robbie had goosebumps. He was shocked to see that a King in Yellow had been referenced in a few manuscripts from the Roman Empire. More thorough perusing revealed references from Ancient Greek, though a bit veiled, as they referred to a sickly monarch in astrology, mainly around the constellation of Taurus or having some veiled connection to mainly Venus, but also Saturn and Mars, due to the planetary resonances of the individual stars themselves. It took a while to see how deep the source material could go, but Robbie became convinced that The King was neither a Roman nor Greek god in origin when the earliest manuscripts kept saying that he came "from the East." It intrigued Robbie that The King never became a part of the Greek Olympian or Titan pantheons when it came to their gods, but he seemed certain the King had only been known to a small number of people in those times. He didn't have a chance to be popular, or to enter any pantheon in the public religions of the day. The texts in Greek weren't numerous, and the passages left the descriptions as short as possible. Maybe The King would have fit in as a mythological figure with Pegasus, the gorgons, the satyrs, nymphs, and other Grecian characters. Harsh and even violent deities only seemed to entice the Greeks more than they repulsed them, though it humored Robbie to think that maybe The King could have been too much for the few acquainted with him in the Mediterranean.

Robbie also found texts preserved from Asia Minor, primarily Caria, which Robbie believed was the location of The King's first devotees. Caria knew The King, just as the Thraceans were said to have known Hekate, or the Chaldeans were believed to have discovered and mapped the astrological hours. The King's cult in Caria couldn't have been that large; one text estimated that it never surpassed fifty people. At some point and time, a member in the group betrayed the mysteries and told about the cult's mythology and practices to others. The same member probably revealed that there was an orally recited play amongst the cult, one that spoke of the world's end in veiled lines drenched with the symbolism of a masquerade party, dances, debauchery, and court politics.

The King in Yellow's enigmatic Carian cult disappeared sometime before the current era.

Beyond the symbolism of the play, Robbie was convinced that The King in Yellow was real. Behind the weird deaths of astronauts in space, magicians in chalk-drawn circles, and random citizens in various pockets of America's major cities, Robbie believed the monarch of the play pulled the strings. The Bull of Heaven, like all of the other constellations, was an intelligent force with its own magical sway over the world. Aldebaran, one of its most malicious stars, had long been driving Earth towards its inevitable destruction. Carcosa was a real and awful place.

Robbie would know- he'd been there. In his dream, no, his *astral projection* that had been so lucid and haunting, he had walked those streets. He saw the wraith denizens of the dark metropolis in those avenues and alleyways. He witnessed the executions that never ended, the collections of bloodstained dead bodies in pits and pools, the treacherous signs that glowed from the walls and surveyed the hellish cityscape with approval.

Robbie prayed he'd never see Carcosa again, that he'd never see *his* world end up like that.

After he finished his toast and wiped the toast away from his palms, Robbie turned off the T.V. Another go at the dissertation was in order. He was excited to finish the passage that had been consuming him those past few months, pages that revolved around his interview with Dr. Edward Manning, a brilliant Classical Greek instructor, philosopher, and grimoire magician.

The dissertation, thick as it was, felt lighter when Robbie picked it up and headed to his room. Being so close to the finish line felt more like a victory than he imagined it would when he first picked this topic. Soon, nights of clacking away on the laptop would be done. He could drink as he stretched out on the hammock in the backyard and forget about the years that weighed him down. Though research into such a topic that he was passionate about proved a great joy, so did the thoughts of rest, an activity sorely needed in Robbie's life.

Besides, he missed his other joy-ritual. His roommate had moved out eight months ago, allowing Robbie to rearrange the guest bedroom and work out some conjurations of his own. He still felt like a newbie to ceremonial magic, even after a decade of dabbling, but Dr. Manning had lit a fire in him. After he finished that paper, he was ready to dive into any magical work that didn't involve pit stops to Carcosa.

*

"So do you believe the practices of this cult could have mirrored any rituals we have records of from the Greeks?" Robbie asked from the digital recording on his laptop. "Say, like the Greek Magical Papyri, for instance."

"As they were influenced by the Chaldeans and Egyptians in much the same way, I would believe so," Dr. Manning answered in the recording. "Much like the cult of Isis influenced tribes in the Middle East and the Mediterranean, the Carian King In Yellow cult shows similarities to Egypt and Chaldea in practice. There seemed to be an invoking and evoking of Taurean spirits, especially from Aldebaran and even Algol."

"And since those were known as harsh stars back in those times," Robbie said, "you'd say that mirrors some of the... damn, I'm trying not to sound like a trendy goth here... dark spirituality of the day? Like the terror found in the Brimo form of Hekate, or the darker aspects of Shiva's Bhairava in India?"

"Their King was an intimidating deity, for sure," said Dr. Manning, "as were their rituals. They gave blood sacrifices, inside and outside of the group. I'm sure you read about that on the DigiWebs and the manuscripts you were able to find. Humans, usually from rival tribes and territories. Enemies. Merchants captured on the road. Traitors."

As Robbie jotted down more notes, he couldn't believe this luck. No matter how many times he listened to the audio, he still couldn't believe that he got to snag an interview with Dr. Edward Manning. Dr. Motherfucking Edward Manning! Robbie had spent many a night studying grimoires Dr. Manning had translated from Ancient Greek, Roman, and other more obscure languages. Manning published books on magic, medicine, alchemy, mathematics, and more. Robbie tried not to geek out during the interview, but he could hear the fanboy run wild in his voice as he listened to the tapes. Oh well, that was okay. Dr. Manning had been kind to him and didn't seem bothered by Robbie's adulation, nor did the professor come off as pompous or elitist. Robbie couldn't believe how down to earth a man could be in the doctor's position, one who probably had to suffer fools anytime he came into contact with everyday people.

That interview gave Robbie all of the pieces he needed to piece this thing together and wrap it up. Dr. Manning had read every manuscript Robbie had been able to read and more. He was even familiar with the DigiWeb forums discussing the King in Yellow, the hysteria that had been built up, how laymen throughout the general population were even starting to put two and two together on where this play, and the threat to humanity, was coming from. If only the Space Program would take that public research seriously. If only the government would take it seriously.

And maybe they did? Who knew?

Robbie pulled his attention back to the recording. Sometimes, the excitement and his ponderings on the material caused his mind to wander, but he would always return. He gripped his pen again, hoping new notes would flow.

"So do you think these dreams I've had align with this material?" Robbie asked from the audio. "The Grecian girl, I mean. You said her dress aligns with the dress of the time, as I found in illustrations."

"Oh, yes," said Dr. Manning. "I have no doubts that she was real. You tapped into her through the astral. Somehow, perhaps by planetary resonances through your chart or because The King is akin to you in some way, your consciousnesses aligned. As she is an agent of the King, she probably exists with him in the world of ideas, the intellectual realm where gods and higher powers reside, outside the confines of space and time. We live in the material realm, and connect to these spirits through the planetary powers, as the planets reside between the world of ideas and the world of man. His star, Alderbaran, grants him the power to connect to us; it's only easier to use his astral powers to send his agents for the dirty work."

Robbie froze. He thought he deleted this part of the audio and deemed it as unimportant to his paper. Personal experiences, though they drove him to tackle this subject in the first place, were unprofessional to handle in the dissertation itself. On top of that, this part of the audio sent chills down his spine; it was too personal, too fucking scary. Robbie thought about stopping the recording, but he could only listen and draw back on the doctor's musings.

"I only fear for you in your connection to this woman and her King," said Dr. Manning. "You admitted that you found her beautiful. Lust remains the strongest vice a malevolent deity can exploit to ensnare and trap the human mind. Even through his agents, once The King has made contact with you and broken through your defenses with the aid of your weaknesses, the connection is permanent. Unbreakable. And in your chart, you had your moon in Taurus, quite close to Alderbaran, yes? The receptive power of the moon would only make you more susceptible, especially since The King usually makes The Yellow Sign appear on the moon to his marked subjects in dreams."

"As it happened in mine." The quiver in Robbie's voice seemed amplified by the recording.

"The King is also not as easy to get rid of as other arcane beings," Dr. Manning continued. "Spirits are usually easy to cast away through a variety of means. Take the classical use of iron and its connection to Mars. All one would need is iron, either in a dagger form or even as loose metal, and it's enough to drive spirits away. The reciting of psalms and the holy names of God, even from the mouth of an areligious person, can banish the most malicious of spirits. Garlic, mugwort, onions- there are so many herbal and vegetable banes that can repel spirits and send them back to their domain. Hell, even consuming fish can drive them away. They hate strong stenches.

"In contrast, The King relishes in the odors, metals, and tools that would banish most menacing apparitions. He scoffs as scriptures no matter how holy and prayers no matter how heartfelt. Songs and prayers of the divine will do nothing for you. He delights in pungent scents, smells of death and corrosion. Whereas most spirits, even the worst ones, prefer to visit a clean room, he likes dirty spaces. He likes unclean people. With that said, even if you cleanse yourself, or purify your person and aura, he does not go away easily once he has you, if at all. Now. This woman. I believe the sign that she greeted you with in your first meeting… you said the dreams started half a decade ago?"

"Yes," Robbie said.

"The finger to the lips," Dr. Manning said, "as you know, is a common sign in occult orders. Masonry. The sign of silence, as occult knowledge should remain hidden. I mean, that's what occult means. Hidden. Secret. The only difference in her sign of silence is that her finger was curved, which mimics the curving angles of the appendages in The King's sign. The opposite hand motion that you saw accompanying the silence gesture, however, is quite unique: rubbing across the neck-"

"-like a dagger slitting a throat," Robbie completed.

Seconds of silence followed.

Dr. Manning continued. "Surely, her vow of silence and whatever knowledge she shared with you is quite serious."

More silence.

"Do you think," Robbie said, "that I could be punished for even discussing these things with you and recording them? My experiences. The dreams. The information outside of what's already public and committed to these discovered manuscripts. I mean, even if I don't release this audio and keep it confidential, do I have reason to fear admonishment?"

"Highly possible, I'm afraid," said Dr. Manning. "Though I'm not the best to ask as I'm not an initiate myself, at least not with anything that has to do with The King in Yellow. Even in my ceremonial work, I've avoided those malevolent stars of Alderbaran, Algol, even the softer and more melancholic Pleaides with a passion. And I'm thankful that they've avoided me. Perhaps the planetary alignment at my birth gives me a different path, for which I won't complain." Dr. Manning sighed. "I'm sorry, I'm drifting from your question. By sharing these things, if she did give you such a severe sign to keep quiet, then yes. You could be punished. At the worst, if she or even The King expected you to share the knowledge by *not* knowing you should keep it secret, you could be rewarded."

More silence.

"Being rewarded is far worse than being punished by The King?"

Dr. Manning gulped louder than he spoke. "Nothing that comes from The King is benevolent in nature, Robert. It would have been better if you'd never received the dreams in the first place. And to be doing a project on it? God, or Gods, help your soul."

*

After the first vision of the beautiful woman, more dreams came over the years.

The woman's visitations were random and sparse at first. Months had passed before he saw her again. She stood over a lake surrounded by fertile vineyards, gazing first at the moon and then at the waters. Across the moon and lake's surface had been The Yellow Sign.

Robbie initially rationalized the second dream as subconscious clutter. The Yellow Sign had been all over the news, in stories that revolved around the ASP and the deaths of astronauts.

Of course, he shouldn't have been surprised that it would appear in his imagination while he slept. As the dreams continued, however, The Sign came more frequently, usually with the woman in tow. The arcane symbol had an inexplicable pull, which only grew stronger with each vision. The woman remained silent, smiling, appearing in a gamut of settings- vineyards, mountains, beaches, caves. She would point and The Sign would present itself in a ferocious glow with a need to be seen and admired.

Each dream drew Robbie to research more. He found the play online and read it front to back. It seemed so theatrical and melodramatic, yet it chilled Robbie to the bone. The unmasking scene felt as if it unmasked his own soul, robbing it of vitality, draining his body to the bone like a ravaged wendigo in some legend native to the American soil…

This legend, however, transcended America. It transcended the world, while Earth seemed caught in the crossfires of something archaic, otherworldly, and insatiable.

Within that first year, the woman in Robbie's dreams would appear in more modern settings- libraries, archival departments at universities, bookstores. Robbie ignored a number of those visions before he finally looked up one of the libraries on the DigiWebs. Shocked to find a matching library name, he drove eight hours away from home and through four states to reach the location. Just as it appeared in the DigiWebs photos, the library looked exactly as it did in his dream, though being there proved more intense of an experience for Robbie. The book that the woman had pointed to in the dream was also on the exact same shelf in the physical world- a small 1895 book, dusty yet well-preserved, entitled *The*

King and His Signs by Robert W. Chambers.

Robbie read that book within that afternoon, well before the library closed. He was fascinated to see The Yellow Sign in a book well before it had become common knowledge to the world. Why wasn't the ASP talking about this? Why weren't politicians and other officials bringing up the book in their televised conferences? Descriptions of the Taurus constellations, its stars, and a secret king that ruled near the star of Aldebaran had never been mentioned on the news. Suggestions that ancient secret cults in Anatolia, right where Turkey existed today, may have worshipped this monarch had remained unknown to Robbie until that day. Surely, it remained unknown to the population at large. Could the answers really be this easy to find?

Robbie no longer held back from visiting the libraries and bookstores that the woman showed him in his dreams. Intrigued as much as he felt scared, he ventured on, driving from one archive to another throughout the states. Some places were hard to gain access to as a graduate student, but once he started working on his doctorate, doors which were once closed to him seemed to open with ease. The older books were in languages he didn't know: Greek, Roman, Aramaic, Hebrew, and Arabic amongst many others. Kind-hearted professors and colleagues helped decipher a number of the works for him, and intrusive questions usually ceased when Robbie explained how important these records were for his dissertation. Sure, they knew he was finding links between some ancient Anatolian cult and the recent King in Yellow craze, but they didn't need to know about the reasons behind his personal interests. They'd all think him to be crazy if he even touched on his dreams.

As he studied the manuscripts and books, taking down notes, Robbie paid attention to the DigiWeb forums and sites as well. Most of the people posting probably had psychological problems of their own, or were perhaps *too* obsessed with the KIY. Some rambled with all sorts of inconsistent and outlandish theories, but the whole thing was outlandish, wasn't it? Even the grounded information that matched other details revolving Aldebaran and its king sounded insane. There was no way for any of it to be taken seriously by the normal public at large, which was probably why these secrets remained untapped, or at least wasn't televised and printed, by the mainstream press at large.

The woman didn't appear in all of Robbie's dreams about The Sign. In one of the most terrifying dreams, the Taurean bull chased him through the cosmos. Its only visible eye, Aldebaran, gleamed with rage, sometimes red, sometimes gold, sometimes that pallid yellow of death, as its horns ripped through the fabric of space. Robbie struggled to maintain a fast speed, winded and filled with panic. He felt the bull could trample or impale him at any second, yet it remained behind him for what felt like hours, perhaps toying with Robbie, knowing it could destroy him any time it wanted to.

Another dream, in which Robbie wandered unaccompanied by the beautiful woman, was in Carcosa. He *knew* it was the famed wicked city, from its tall black spires that overshadowed the cracked and uneven streets, to the hordes of ghosts that wandered through the evil metropolis like a discarded graveyard. Smells of rotting meat and blood filled the area. The chiming of a haunted bell called him to the castle at the center of Carcosa, and he could not deny its magnetic strength, floating towards it in his astral form past the gates that parted for him, up obsidian stairs and into darkness as thick as night itself. The throne room waited, guarded by mammoth guards in pallid armor, their ebony spears crossed as they refused entry.

That dream taunted Robbie most of all. So many secrets revealed, yet the king remained veiled to him, denied, off-limits.

As Robbie's research into The King and his realm increased, he couldn't help but feel a strong interest in the occult as a whole. In Robbie's childhood, he'd shown an interest in the paranormal, things that were unseen, ghosts, psychic phenomenon, and conspiracies, but he believed he'd long outgrown such things. He'd become a rational atheistic adult, a college graduate with the interest to continue his education and perhaps become a professor one day. With a major in Philosophy and a masters in Religion, Robbie believed he would merely teach logic classes or religious history. This King in Yellow business, however, made him reconsider his purpose if he ever became a teacher. Perhaps he was not so pragmatic and grounded, after all.

Dr. Edward Manning's books had only furthered Robbie's interests. The doctor was brilliant, and it was refreshing to see a well-educated professor in a materialistic, anti-spiritual modern era treat the occult in such a serious way. As not only an academic but an experienced occultist, Dr. Manning spoke of spirits and ceremonial magic in a matter-of-fact way and shared his experiences without shame. It made magic real for Robbie, and while he respected and admired other specialists in the craft, Dr. Manning stood out with his erudite expertise and made Robbie want to throw all of his Richard Dawkins books in the trash.

If not for Dr. Edward Manning, Robbie would have stayed on the armchairs, reading about magic yet too afraid to practice it. Dr. Manning inspired Robbie to find places in the woods, to follow grimoiric instructions and cast his own circles. Soon, Robbie called up spirits of his own as he conducted his rituals and tested his aptitude for the magic arts. He conjured mercurial spirits to help him find more papers and grimoires for his research and occult practice. Just as woman in his dreams had done, they brought him more books through mysterious ends: boxes dropped outside his front door, books mailed from random librarians who looked at his accounts and thought he might enjoy something, heavy tombs of manuscripts that were said to be lost yet appeared in his car or during a walk in the woods. If not for the magic he encountered with the woman herself, such literary finds would be seen as coincidences instead of the result of true spiritual communication. Robbie knew the spirits were responsible. He saw them consciously and externally, through his own physical eyes, during ritual. He got exactly what he asked for. Luckily, no blood contracts had to be drawn and all requests to own his soul had been turned down, yet just the recitation of God's various names in Hebrew and Greek were enough to get the spirits to do what he wanted.

Then again, even if they wanted his soul and he gave it to them, would they be able to claim it? If Dr. Manning's words were correct, then The King in

Yellow may have already owned Robbie.

Robbie tried not to think of that. Conjuring other spirits and his growing interest in ritual helped distract Robbie from the horrid possibility that The King in Yellow haunted him. Even if the woman came to him and showed him The King's secrets, that didn't mean he was owned by the monarch, did it? Hell, he hadn't even seen him. The King Himself remained a mystery. Even in his research, in writing this paper and outlining the history surrounding the monarch and his play, his own essence hadn't been compromised.

But she came to him. Even if he ignored her, if he hadn't done anything with the knowledge she offered, The King could have claimed him as a possession. But for what end?

*

Dr. Manning's death didn't surprise Robbie.

Despite the lack of surprise, the photos in the press upset him. How invasive to show the doctor's corpse and the scene of death on news sites and papers! With all the work they'd done to suppress the alien documents and artifacts, it seemed odd that showing an old academic lying dead in the middle of a chalk-drawn circle didn't seem like much of a journalistic violation. The poor old man wore his white hooded cloak, and Robbie recognized the protective circle, drawn on his basement floor to protect the man from any spiritual harm, was the *Ouroboros,* a snake-figure that represented the infinite universe with its tail in its mouth. Many a magician used the ouroboros as a protective circle in occult workings, while others used a simple line with names of the divine around it.

The press claimed that Dr. Manning died of a heart attack while in the middle of one of his magic procedures, something the academic was well known for doing as an occultist with many magic-based publications under his belt. Robbie, however, knew better.

Something crossed the circle. Something killed him.

Drawn in front of the circle was the ever-important triangle. While the Ouroboros was constructed with a 9-foot radius, the triangle was significantly smaller, no more than 3 feet tall from its base to its tip. The purpose of the triangle was to contain any spirit that appeared and force them to tell the truth. The triangle, as a symbol, had many associations- harmony, balance, law and order. Whatever had been conjure would have been drawn to that triangular prison. Along with the circle, the incense, and the holy water Robbie knew the doctor would not neglect to consecrate the space, no spirit was supposed to do the magician any harm.

The King in Yellow wasn't like any other spirits, however, nor were his minions. If anything could break past the barriers of the doctor's protection, they surely could.

No blood had been drawn and there was no sign of bruising, except for the unmistakable marking on the doctor's back that they had found. The pictures Robbie found of the autopsy a week later, which he had to dive deep into the Digi-Web to find, only confirmed his suspicions. The King would leave his mark *someway,* and he did, with those pallid curves and hooks etched deep across the doctor's back.

The doctor had been initiated in death.

Or maybe he'd been a part of The King's cult all of that time, playing as if he were an outsider to Robbie's experiences and dreams. The possibility only seemed stronger when Robbie did more digging on the DigiWebs about the doctor. Never had Robbie thought much about the Doctor's birthdate, where he was born or when until now. He grabbed the information and went to an astrology site, then plugged in all of the details. At 64 years old, the doctor's sun was in Cancer, his rising was Capricorn-

Robbie's heart missed a beat as he saw the doctor's moon sitting in Taurus, just a degree higher than his own. The moon was smack-dab on Alderbaran, receptive and bright.

Robbie closed his laptop. He didn't even get far from the couch before he threw up all over his living room carpet. He didn't like the synchronicity, coincidental or substantial. His body felt drained of energy, vertigo seizing his brain as he spaced over the kitchen sink. His body grew hot and fevered.

He tried to rid his mind of the few positions he had seen in the doctor's chart. Only the moon over Aldebaran refused to be forgotten. In bed, long after he'd thrown out his carpet and scrubbed the floorboards and sink, Robbie laid restless as that moon remained transfixed in his mind. Over its silvery luminescence, The Yellow Sign burned over its cratered countenance.

As The Yellow Sign emitted its golden flames, the moon turned blood-red in Robbie's mind.

Robbie tried to rest, but The Yellow Sign and its crimson moon kept him up that night, as well as the night after that. All Robbie could do was pray that his obsession would go away, that he could let the doctor rest in peace. He feared that every prayer went to the wrong deity and his efforts to break free were in vain, but it was all he could do. Stubborn and as restless as

Robbie, perhaps more, The Yellow
Sign refused to be banished.

*

Robbie couldn't get visions of The
Sign on Dr. Manning's back out of his
head. He knew that marking well, not
only because The Yellow Sign could be
seen all over the media, but because the
woman in his dreams wore it on her
back as well.

He'd only see her back once. About a
year into the visions, she called him
back to the banks of the lake where
they'd first met. She sat on its edge
with her feet in the water as wind
rushed through the vineyards, making
the lake's surface ripple in soft waves.
He came to her and sat beside her.
Never had she appeared to him so
lucidly. He reached out to her cheek
and touched her for the first time

She touched his cheek in return. Her
hands were elegant and slender. Her
palms were soft. She must have

belonged to a noble family, free from toiling the land. She looked into Robbie's eyes, her gaze longing.

They kissed. Their arms embraced, their hands trailing each other's backs. He could tell, as his fingers traced her dress, that something had been engraved along and around her spine. The fabric was thin, and the deep groves along the flesh underneath surprised him. A flood of confusion and sorrow went through him. Empathy rose as Robbie's intuition suggested that she wasn't as well off as he thought. Perhaps she was a slave with scars to bear. Perhaps some horrid incident had disfigured her from behind, or a jealous lover had been cruel to her long before an age where the rights of women were taken seriously, if such an age had ever come.

By the time they stripped and he saw The Sign branded on her, he still wasn't prepared to see it. Not only was The

Sign skin-deep, but it glowed, golden at points, sallow at others. A gravitational vacuum sucked at Robbie's life-force, and he had to release the woman. His body started to inch away.

She grabbed him. She kissed him with more intensity, more passion, as they faced each other nude with only the moon and the water to bear vigil over them. The wind howled about them and an unnaturally cold, savage, primordial breeze began to cover them. The woman's kisses graced his neck and chest.

This was not sexy. No beauty came of this make-out session. What started as passionate and sensuous now petrified Robbie to the core. He tried to shake himself from the woman's grasp but he lost feeling in his body. Soon, he felt limp in her arms as she cradled him, kissed him, sliding against his lap with the grip and strength of a possessed Olympian bodybuilder.

A burning sensation pierced Robbie's back from the center, curling outwards in a series of directions. He hollered as the woman continued to kiss him along his face, massaging his arms and sides, refusing to let him go.

Robbie woke up. Sweat covered his sheets and pillow. Fear erupted in his eyes as he stared out, thankful to see his room around him. That lake and its surrounding vineyards seemed far behind.

After he stood in front of his bathroom mirror and inspected his back with an opposing hand mirror, Robbie breathed a sigh of relief. The Sign had not manifested itself on his true back. It had all been a dream, a passing night terror. He could put the night behind him and move on.

But the night had never left him. That terrifying dream lingered in Robbie's mind for years. The sight of The Yellow Sign on Dr. Manning's back only brought back the memory, and what had been ignored as a mere nightmare presented itself in reality with the poor professor's death.

Had The Sign been there before? Had it come with his passing? The question drove Robbie to the edge of his sanity. Perhaps Dr. Manning had been chosen by The King long ago and didn't want to add to Robbie's woes, knowing his own end was at hand. He spoke as an outsider, as one who'd merely read and studied up on the marked victims of The King, in the possible attempt of giving Robbie some hope. *Perhaps* Robbie could avoid an inescapable fate of being at the whim of The King. *Perhaps* the information behind The King in those written documents and artifacts weren't set in stone. *Perhaps.*

With Dr. Manning's death, Robbie saw no hope. If Dr. Manning had gone years with The Yellow Sign in his flesh, maybe even decades… then

Robbie could have a great deal of time before he met his own end. Besides, the mark vanished as soon as he woke from that disturbing nightmare. But what if Dr. Manning had awoken from his own dreams as well, living while hanging on his own thread of hope, only to have the sign reappear on his physical flesh once his body expired?

Robbie couldn't think of these things, yet they were *all* he could think about. The dissertation had finally been completed, the main thing that had held Robbie's attention all those years, and now his inspiration had been slain. The most important person he'd interviewed for the paper was no more, at least on this planet. Dr. Manning could be forced to dance in the courts of The King in Yellow for all Robbie knew, howling with other wraiths enslaved to the castle's necromantic energies.

Dr. Manning was gone. Robbie thought about what he needed to do now that his dissertation had been completely. He'd turn it in to his professors, have them read over it, share it with the department and prepare it for publication if it had passed their standards. Soon, it could be a searchable resource in the same libraries and databases where he found his own cited material. Others who wanted to look deeper into the history of The King in Yellow and his earliest recorded worshippers could do so.

After Robbie built a valuable reputation in the academic world as a scholar and even a professor himself, he could think about printing the more raw material he'd accumulated in his more personal journals and notes. The first-hand experiences, the dreams, the woman and the bull, his conversation with Dr. Manning and the others. That could happen in perhaps another half a decade or more, depending on how many moves he made in teaching and

hobnobbing with the university elites.
Maybe the world wouldn't be
destroyed by that time to build a
collegiate career and share those more
intimate experiences.

Time would tell, though by the recent
events, the odds of more time did not
look favorable. There would be hell to
pay, and pain, if an ultimate end was
not right around the corner. Either way,
even in a hopeless world, all Robbie
had was hope.

*

A month after Dr. Manning died,
Robbie saw the woman again.

Robbie stood in the dark for a long
time and didn't know where he was. He
knew he was sleeping, and assumed
that while conscious, he must have
been in some deep REM sleep without
any dreams. He couldn't feel his body,
probably due to sleep paralysis. But
soon, from above, blue lights appeared

like stars and offered some illumination.

Robbie was in a cave. Before him, he saw her, looking upwards as the stars showed themselves. Soon, the constellation of Taurus was visible on that ceiling. More constellations emanated into view, but the bull remained prevalent.

The star of Aldebaran grew, overriding the other stars. The planets of Aldebaran became visible. The King's realm consumed the ceiling. Carcosa's streets stretched out before them.

Golden and pale-yellow lights illuminated the cave's passage, right above the woman.

The woman screamed. She saw things that Robbie could not see, heard things he couldn't hear. Her eyes opened, and the same pallid light glowed from her orbs as her dress split and ripped to shreds.

The Yellow Sign etched itself, curve by curve, on the poor woman's back with golden fire.

Robbie wanted to run towards her and give aid, but he couldn't move. Hell, he couldn't feel his body. As some formless and stuck spirit, he could only serve as a spectator, a witness.

You are my true witness, as I am yours.

That wasn't right. A woman's voice spoke in his mind. *Hers.* He'd never heard her speak before this point, and though she spoke in an ancient form of Greek, a language Robbie was quite limited in no matter the era, he *understood* her... linguistically, at least. The implied meaning evaded him, however. He knew what she told him word for word, though he didn't know what being his witness entailed. His witness. Her witness. Witnesses to what? *For* what?

The light consumed the passage. Soon, Robbie saw another section of the cave, some wide cavern room filled with statues and partiers in masks. They conversed with laughter, drank wine and gorged on food. One man looked nervous and upset. By his dress and facial features, Robbie assumed he was the only Grecian of this Turkish-looking bunch, perhaps even related to the woman as their noses, eyes, and mouths were so similar.

The woman appeared in the room with a pallid glow, yet she was not in her human form. Her hooves slammed into the rock-forged floor. Her snout breathed scarlet fire. Her horns shined as she gave a horrid, demonic roar, stars of blue, red, and white decorating her golden steer body.

Even as the partygoers caught sight of the woman and began to run, dropping their gauntlets and plates, it was too late for them. The bull, burning in a fiery glow, charged into the room. Robbie could feel the woman's essence deep within that animal, but knew that He dominated its animation and form, that He was in control.

The bull's horns impaled bodies. Its fiery hooves trampled over legs, stomachs, and arms. Internal parts were made external as intestines, livers, and hearts flew left and right, lit aflame by the fires of the bull. Masked men and women screamed as their precious cult, preserved for hundreds if not thousands of years, found itself leveled in seconds.

The Grecian man remained. He cowered as the bull stared into his eyes. There was some sympathy from the beast, some compassion, which held it back from its final kill.

The compassion did not last for long. *He* required these sacrifices. The Grecian cried out in vain as he was mauled, ripped to shreds by the horns and teeth of the angry bull. His blood and burning organs mixed with the many around him as his bones were shattered and peeled back, discarded, leveled to broken, disordered debris.

Soon after the last man's destruction, the glow of the bull died out in smoldered flames. The beast evaporated into spoke. The woman rose from its disintegration, fumes rising from her skin, as she looked around in shock and dismay. She crumbled before the blazed pulp of the Grecian man as other carrion burned around her. Terror consumed her visage. As she lifted her hands to her mouth, appalled by what she had done, the voice of The King echoed through the cave.

Your grandfather did well, said The King. *As did you. Now, out into the world. Preserve the play by memory. Write it and store it in secret. The generations of man shall continue. Chosen ones will reinterpret and change it under my instruction. The day shall be preserve. But those many days are beyond you now, my loyal devotee. Do your work. You will dance in my court soon enough.*

*

As Robbie awaited the approval of his dissertation, he focused on his magical practice.

Since he finished the paper, he reread the books he owned from Dr. Manning, bought some new ones, and studied new material. He acquainted himself with various herbs for incense workings with different planetary spirits, studied old cultures and philosophies, soaked in different approaches to invocation and evocation. With the spare room he now had in his home, which he could dedicate entirely to magic, he had more time on his hands to try as many tasks as possible. Some operations worked, others didn't. He didn't go for anything outlandish when it came to ritual work; his favorite ceremonies revolved around acquiring new knowledge. He had no need to ensnare a lover or to ruin an enemy.

The distractions that the grimoires had to offer couldn't pull his mind away from The King in Yellow for too long. On another Wednesday, he stood in his white robe at the center of an Ouroboros circle with the 72 divine names written around him. Robbie exercised patience while he waited for his chosen being to appear in the triangle that he had drawn in front of the circle.

A voice vibrated through his skull.

Make The King manifest in the flesh.

His voice. The King's. He remembered it from the dream of the cave. The sound of it in the waking world brought no comfort. Robbie broke out into a sweat in the middle of the circle. Flashbacks of Dr. Manning's corpse lying in the center of his own circle made Robbie's heart race as cold shocks met his arm. He dropped his ceremonial sword.

Make The King manifest in the flesh.

No incense could bar Him. Not enough holy water in the world could be splashed around the walls, nor could the corners of the room be smudged just right to seal Him out. There were no songs that He would not find pleasing, no scripture that could banish Him, no ritual that could drown Him out. Once He marked you, you were His.

"God help me." Robbie tried to keep his legs straight, to stay as close to the center of the circle as possible. He feared leaving the room, though he knew there was nowhere to go that was safe, in or out of the sphere. "Please shield me from that monster. Please."

Laughter vibrated through the room.

"Make The King manifest in the flesh."

His ears heard it this time. No longer in Robbie's head, The King seemed to be coming from the left, the right, from above and below. Robbie looked around with fright. No. This couldn't be the end. He had a doctorate to earn. He had classes to teach, seminars to attend. If he expanded beyond his university, he could become an expert in the fields of philosophy, religion, and classical cultures. He could go on speaking tours, have books published, do CarlConvos on the DigiWebs with PowerPoints and a funny catchphrase prepared.

The magician must establish his authority, Robbie remembered from one of the doctor's books. *Do not make friends with them. Do not play nice. In the scheme of things, under the Gods, under the angels, and even under us as men, daemons were created to do our desires. Not the other way around. Make no blood pacts. Give no power to them. Own your power, and make them step into the triangle, where no lie can be told.*

Robbie pointed his index towards the triangle at the front of his circle. "Step into the triangle. Do no harm onto me. This is my space, and I command you to listen!"

A hand grabbed Robbie's leg as fire roared under him.

Robbie shouted as he looked down and saw a man's arm extending from a golden flicker that rose from the floor, right in the center of the circle, as that hand gripped his pant leg beneath Robbie's white robe. With a strong tug, a head and shoulders ascended from the floor's surface and stared up at Robbie. The man wore sores that popped on his burnt and sagging skin, which clung for dear life against the muscles and bone of his face. Those pleading eyes watered as The Yellow Sign glowed upon his forehead.

"Father," said a voice in an ancient form of Greek. "Why did you wander so far from me?"

Robbie looked out to the circle and saw the beautiful woman from his dreams, her dress elegant and smooth under the candlelight that surrounded the room. He understood her! Not a word of English had been uttered… yet he understood the dead form of her language as clear as day. Undoubtedly the magic of The King in Yellow had penetrated the space and given him such an uncanny gift, breaking the language barrier.

"You will understand that we do not entertain triangles," said the woman. "Nor do we allow your circle to separate you from us, initiate. Our King won't allow it. You are His, as am I."

Behind the woman was another familiar figure. The points of curved knives and swords riddled the man's tortured flesh as nails had been driven in his arms and legs. Blood trailed from his hands and knees as he walked on all fours. His eyes stared out to Robbie with sorrow, trembling as tears ran along the new scars on his face. A tight golden collar choked him as blood ran beneath its circular edge, the skin around it bruised in black, blue, and red patches.

"Dr. Manning," Robbie breathed.

The woman looked down to the doctor, then patted him on the head. "I pray you're not jealous? I do care deeply for you both. The King brought us all together. He is merciful."

Dr. Manning broke down in wet sobs.

"Time and space is less of a factor in Carcosa," said the woman in her clear Greek tongue. "Not obsolete, but fluid under the whim of His Grace. That's how He connected us. We should be so thankful that He saw our usefulness. I know you fear the death. The pain. The decay. As did we all, brother. Fear not. You will get used to it. You will praise Him and you will know that you suffer for the preservation of The King. For the preservation and expansion of Carcosa."

Robbie frowned. Would she understand him as well as he understood her?

"What purpose does Dr. Manning serve to The King?" asked Robbie. "What purpose do I serve?"

"We all serve the ushering in of a new era for our beautiful solar systems," said the woman. "Bridging the gaps between Aldebaran and Earth. My father fulfilled his mission of moving the gospel of The King beyond the borders of Caria to the swine of the world. But we who are chosen are lucky to stand on a humble pedestal above them."

The burnt cadaver snarled in Robbie's circle, tightening his grip as his nails stabbed around Robbie's ankle.

"I brought about one of many essential group sacrifices," the woman continued, "as you saw first-hand. I gave to our beloved King His most devoted cult, men and women who did any and everything for Him. They ushered in the dawning of a new age, and it was my privilege to give them their reward! They maintained His secrets here on Earth for centuries, until they were no longer needed to be secret, of course." The woman reached into her dress and pulled out a dagger with a black handle, slamming it into the top of the professor's cranium and making him scream with agony. "From there, I was sent out into the world as the cult's sole survivor. I made more sacrifices. When He was satisfied with that, I wrote an early form of the play as it had been orally dictated to me and gave it to a Persian sorcerer chosen by our King. I then committed suicide and took my position in the ballrooms of The King's palace. You'll see it soon, brother, and participate as well. The formations. The pivots. The spins. Our dancing is so glorious."

The professor screamed as the woman twisted the knife in his skull.

"Please don't do that," Robbie said with a raised hand.

"Many came through the ages and stored the play away," she continued, "keeping it secret, changing it from time to time to fit with the coming seasons of change. The play has seen the insides of pyramids, of temples and churches. It's been housed in the Library of Alexandria. Monks rewrote it during the Medieval Ages and the Renaissance. The Vatican, the Louvre, hidden rooms in The British Library and elsewhere- the play has known many a home. The King knew that the time for the play to become public knowledge would soon approach, that it would shift the world, and prepare all for His coming."

Dr. Manning coughed blood on the floor.

"This one has reinterpreted various grimoires for decades," the woman said, "slipping in little procedures and details that would make it easier for The King to come to this less dense plane. As polluted and vile as Earth is, would you believe that its less adulterated frequencies were still hard for Our King to penetrate in order to manifest physically and fully here? War, filth, and disease are constants in this world, but He required more for the appropriate entryway. We've accomplished that now, thanks to Brother Grim War here and you, and many others around the world who have performed rituals from his grimoire translations. Your dissertation was an important operation as well, a historical document that will stand the test of time and allow the enslaved denizens of this world to remember who first established contact with our beloved King. They'll know who blessed them with this great fate."

"The Carians were truly the first then," Robbie said.

"Not the first to make contact," said the woman, "but the first to be brave enough to build a mystery cult around Him. To do the Great Work necessary to invoke Him and bring Him here, to establish the seeds of His law on Earth. For our brothers and sisters, we should forever be thankful. Oh, how He will bless you!"

Robbie cowered as he heard Dr. Manning moan in agony. He did *not* want those blessings. "Take this mark away. Let me live. Please."

"As if you have a choice?" the woman asked.

Robbie bit his bottom lip. There was no way to kill time, no hope in running away. "What's your name?"

"You will learn that," said the woman, "if The King finds you worthy. Your primer education was only finished. Your initiation has just begun. Know me as Cassilda, sweet Robert… we shall soon see if you are a brother or just a mere sacrifice."

The woman's flesh began to melt and bubble about her face and limbs. Hair fell in small clumps from her scalp.

The room started to shake. Magical tools and candles fell off of tables and onto the floor.

"I don't want this!" Robbie shouted.

"It's not about what we want," the woman said, boils rising from her ruined flesh. "It's about what *He* wants!"

The last candle went out. The rumbling room went dark as the woman laughed.

Robbie lost his footing and fell to the ground. As if startled, the corpse beneath him bit his arm and slashed at Robbie's legs, drawing blood. Robbie screamed as he tried to kick and push the man away.

The ceiling collapsed. Something heavy hit Robbie on the head, then everything went dark.

*

Robbie moaned as he looked up, his legs crushed beneath rubble as blood poured from his scalp and down his forehead. Through weak and blurry eyes, Robbie looked around. The homes of his suburban neighborhood smoldered beneath fires, dust clouds dispersing as smoke rose towards the sky. Screams erupted from various directions as an army of swordsmen in pale-yellow armor slaughtered helpless victims.

The shrieking and sights of blood churned Robbie's stomach, though it only added to his own pain instead of distracting him from it. He vomited in a harsh wave that burned his throat, a trail of blood with pink pulp spewing from his guts. He moaned in grief, as his eyes slowly regained their clarity; the world was no longer blurry, though he wished it could remain opaque. Robbie didn't want to see the deaths and destruction, and he certainly didn't want to see *Him.*

But there He was, worse than the forums of the DigiWebs had described Him, worse than the American Space Program classified records had speculated, than anything the play could reveal or those archeology records could decode. He was humanoid for sure, but He stood at what must have been nine feet tall. As

His pallid cape draped from his sickly-yellow armor, His breastplate and the forehead of His helmet bore His sign. The burnt corpse that had once been in Robbie's circle squirmed on His gore-drenched spear and looked into His eyes with great terror.

Robbie looked down and saw, from the parts of the cracked floor that he could see from spaces in the rubble, that he was still in his circle as well.

All in vain, he thought as blood ran from his forehead, nose, and mouth. *Suffering the same end as Dr. Manning.*

Robbie's eyes didn't have to lift far to see Dr. Manning's blade-littered head crushed under The King's boot. In some cruel luck, the doctor survived with that smashed cranium, his eyes bulged out as his tongue hung. Various clumps of his splattered brain matter pulsated on the ground.

"Blood sacrifices for Your Grace," The King said in a booming yet calm voice, though it brought more chaos than tranquility. "Blood sacrifices for Carcosa."

The King pulled His staff out of the burnt corpse with great force. The slaughtered cadaver stumbled for a moment, but soon stood upright, lifeless yet animated by that pallid force which now reflected off of his eyes. He regurgitated more blood, letting it splatter upon the concrete in volumes before he gained better footing. Once stable, he looked to The King and bowed his head.

"The stench of this world," said The King as he looked around with a sneer on his sallow face. "The filth. The contamination. It is beautifully imperfect, and yet it pales in such great contrast to the majesty of My Carcosa. You should see it, thrall. Ever defiled. Ever corroded and decrepit. Always dead Aldebaran." He pressed the spear's sharp point against the living cadaver's face and drew blood from its chin. "If it takes dozen nights of slaughter and the accumulation of death... a hundred nights, a thousand... I will make your world like My own. I will make your star system as beautiful as Mine. Raining blood. Cultivated flesh. Altars of devastation and savagery. Choruses of screams. Forever and ever, amen."

Robbie cried. The tears poured and brought no comfort, no end. He should have died. He should have fucking died! That luxury remained denied to him. His legs refused to move.

The King noticed him, or perhaps He knew Robbie had been watching Him the entire time. His cape flapped behind Him, long as the mirrored constellations danced on its fabric. He shook His spear and it transformed into a sword with a golden flash. That short illumination sent waves of disease and agony through the area, ripping on a radius that consumed Robbie. He didn't want to be here. He didn't want to feel anymore, to encounter any other horrors.

"You there, initiate," said The King. "Why did you pursue the mysteries?" His sword's tip touched Robbie's nose. "Robert McCray. You received My signs, did you not?"

Robbie's eyes rolled back in his head, though he did not command them to do so. Memories of the dreams returned. That scary bull that pursued him through the cosmos. The evil city filled with ghosts and dead bodies. That accursed sign. And it had all started with dreams of *her.*

"You have a witness," said The King. "She vouched for you." He turned around, looking at the rubble of a devastated building. "Chara, Sister Midnight, Vessel of the Bull! Come forth. Your initiate- do you speak for him now?"

A ripple of shadow erupted from before the rubble. A woman appeared from the portal of darkness, her skin pale and yellow, riddled with cracks, warts, and tumors. Her hair hung in clumps from her swollen head, her eyes staring with gray orbs as bruised hallow bags imploded against the skin beneath them, drawn to her gaunt face. She wore blood as lipstick and eyeshadow, as blush and hair dye against tresses that may have been brown at one point. Now, her hair was a terrible mesh of gray and scarlet in a gamut of saturations. A plant foreign to earth, purple and thorny, crowned her head. Wafts of centuries-old blood and shit mixed well with The King's own rancid odor.

She was not like she had been in Robbie's dreams.

The woman replied in a language Robbie didn't know. It sounded like something from the Mediterranean, yet old. Very old. The ability to understand her had been taken away, perhaps momentarily. With The King's grace...

The King looked at the man, humored by his bewilderment. "You lust after her. Still. A soul's connection granted in your devotion for me." He looked to Chara. "And she still lusts for you. She wishes for you to dance with her in My halls. You shall meet her brother, a noble hero, and many others. Men and women of Caria, Chaldea, Greece and Italy. Devotees from Egypt and Nubia, India and Nepal, your precious America. Loyal worshippers from your world and Mine. Carcosans who've known My dance from the beginning of Aldebaran's glow. She still vouches for you, child of beasts. She believes you will still fit in My play. The cosmic dance of eternal decay, of things in and out, the blood and the way."

"Please kill me." Robbie didn't care how weak he sounded, how the words bubbled out of his mouth with the strength of a mewing lamb, how his body quivered. "I don't want to live like this. I don't care what you think or say. I don't lust for that filthy corpse! I don't want a place in your realm!"

"No," said The King. "Of course, you don't want to live. You want to decay. To die. To know the forever, the eternal promise of corrosion. And now you're here. This is it. Here with me. A death most rapturous. Most rewarding and enlightening."

"Not like this, please," Robbie sobbed. "Not conscious. Not in pain."

"What did you think it would be like, Robert?" asked The King. "A dull promise of sleep and emptiness? No sights? No amusements? No purpose or work? You are my devotee. You *must* work. And the work, like the light I've bestowed upon you, is endless."

Robbie heard something soar high above him. He looked up to the sky.

Spacecraft he'd seen on the news for the past few years zoomed into Earth's atmosphere, one by one, and then hovered in wait. The American Space Program and the press deemed those crafts ancient; they operated now. The ships intimidated Robbie with their size, bronze and golden shells that emitted the pale-yellow aura of their King. Robbie imagined the ones who manned the craft to be the dead, perhaps in ghostly or skeletal forms, drained of life yet loyal in their necromantic states with fingers at the control boards, ready to do as their King demanded.

Agony surged across Robbie's back. Hooks and curves spread out from his spine in gold flames. He screamed as the mark cut deep and The King stood over him.

"All hail The King in Yellow!" exclaimed Sister Midnight.

Printed in Great Britain
by Amazon

52084578R00099